If it wasn't bad enough that he had to worry about cops, now civilians were after him too...

It was the kind of thing Karpis's new nightmares were made of. Even though the feds had let him walk free, there was still the police and sheriffs in the podunk towns who would easily think that Public Enemy Number One had escaped without anyone even knowing. He knew that the kind of people who played cops and robbers were the same kind of people on both sides of the fence. There was no way of knowing that the fellow who had smiled and walked away was not running for a phone booth, hoping his name would be mentioned in the newspaper article announcing that Alvin Karpis had been recaptured.

About two tables away, another customer had not blown the incident off quite as cavalierly as Karpis had hoped. Cat the Bounty Hunter was a legend throughout the Midwest, having brought in some of the most wanted criminals in the region's history. Bob Feta was a two-time loser, a cat burglar who began using his skills to capture fugitives using false identities to sequester themselves in high-rise luxury apartments. At six foot, 210 pounds, Feta had the size and fighting skills to take out the criminals he hunted down. He knew Karpis, Campbell, and Doc were in Alcatraz and Fred was six feet under, but these fellows were dead ringers and they had to be playing an angle somewhere.

Amidst rumors of a conspiracy by the Axis powers to diminish America's capacity to engage in hostilities, the FBI is called into action. Special Agent Chess Power is empowered by Deputy Director Melvin Purvis to put together a plan to thwart the efforts of a mysterious team known as the Triad. Power heads out to Alcatraz Island and enlists the aid of criminal genius Alvin Karpis in return for his parole. Karpis agrees on condition that his partners Fred and Doc Barker and Harry Campbell are included in the deal. Power agrees, and the game of cat and mouse soon begins.

KUDOS for *The Triad*

In *The Triad* by John Dizon, Alvin Kapris is let out of Alcatraz in 1938 to help the FBI track down three foreign agents in the US, here to assassinate high-ranking political and military personnel in order to keep the US from entering into WWII. Armed with an abundance of weapons, his three partners in crime—Fred and Doc Barker and Harry Campbell, and a fair amount of Irish luck, Karpis sets about finding the Triad assassins. Of course, having a number of organized crime connections doesn't hurt either. Karpis's motives, of course, are not completely altruistic, however. After all, in no other country in the world could organized crime flourish so easily, so the American way of life is something he wants to preserve. The story has a hint of the paranormal in the form of dreams of the future, which both Kapris and Fred have, but for the most part, it's a solid historical thriller with an intriguing plot and endearing characters who, despite being bank robbers and thugs, step up when their country calls. ~ *Taylor Jones, Reviewer*

The Triad by John Reinhard Dizon is a historical thriller, set in pre-WW2 America in 1938. The Axis Powers send a group of assassins, known as the Triad, to assassinate important political and military targets in America, hoping to cripple the US's ability to interfere with Hitler's plans for world domination. Going with the concept that it takes a crook to catch one, the FBI offers mob-boss Alvin (Ray) Karpis, currently serving time in Alcatraz, parole for his services in hunting down and eliminating the Triad. Karpis agrees to the deal, provided the FBI also includes his associates Harry Campbell and Doc and Fred Barker, also in prison in Alcatraz—well, all except one, who's supposed to be dead. With his partners at his side, Karpis starts a nationwide manhunt using his mob connections, while dodging bounty hunters and concerned citizens who are certain that Karpis has escaped from Alcatraz and is on the loose. I loved the characters, especially Carole and Doc, both of which are clueless and remind me of Betty White's character Rose Nylund on *The Golden Girls*. With delightful characters, a strong and complicated plot with plenty of twists and turns to keep you on your toes, *The Triad* is an exciting and entertaining read. ~ *Regan Murphy, Reviewer*

THE
TRIAD

John Reinhard Dizon

A Black Opal Books Publication

GENRE: POSTMODERNIST/HISTORICAL MYSTERY/THRILLER

THE TRIAD
Copyright © 2016 by John Reinhard Dizon
Cover Design by Marcha Fox
All cover art copyright © 2016
All Rights Reserved
Print ISBN: 978-1-626944-30-5

First Publication: MARCH 2016

Published by Black Opal Books **http://www.blackopalbooks.com**

THE
TRIAD

CHAPTER 1

May 1938:

Chess Power felt as if the Queen Mary had come in when he landed a job with the FBI. Financially, he had gone from comparative rags to considerable riches, having struggled through the Great Depression since 1929. It was seven years of bad luck, and he had been living hand-to-mouth as a lawyer until the Federal Bureau of Investigation began hiring in 1935. He was among those selected, and he voluntarily transferred from Kansas City to Chicago where he reported to the Special Agent in Charge, Melvin Purvis.

Melvin was a Southern dandy whose star was ascending rapidly by favor of the Director, J. Edgar Hoover. Chess was determined to hang onto Melvin's coat-tails as tight as he could. He was unaware that Purvis, the most celebrated agent in the history of the Bureau, had become a David to Hoover's King Saul paranoia. Hoover had grown insanely jealous over Melvin having killed John Dillinger, Baby Face Nelson, and Pretty Boy Floyd in succession. Though Purvis was sidelined as Hoover was set up to personally arrest the last of the Public Enemies, Alvin "Ray" Karpis, J. Edgar still nursed a grudge and had secretly sworn to take down his own golden boy.

Melvin was under the assumption that this assignment was going to secure his star at the top of the tree. He was told by Hoover that a national security directive had empowered the FBI to handle this case, and this could very well make or break the fledgling agency should they fail in their task. He was also told that he would have to rely on unknown agents who had not gotten any publicity during the FBI's War on Crime. The mission depended on utmost secrecy for its success, and the FBI itself could not be publicly connected to any phase of the operation.

Melvin's secretary politely asked Chess to wait as she announced the visitor on the intercom. She herself had gained a measure of celebrity as having interceded on behalf of Billie Frechette as she was being tortured by FBI agents seeking the whereabouts of John Dillinger. Chess was one of the hunters and gatherers during those glory days, following up leads on obscure gunmen holding up banks in farm towns from Oklahoma to Arkansas. When he considered all those who were wounded or killed under gunfire of the public enemies, however, Chess had no complaints.

"Chester Power." Melvin came around his desk to shake hands after having him sent in.

Chess was not a particularly big man at five feet, nine inches and one-hundred-fifty pounds, yet he towered over his diminutive boss who was a mere five feet, four inches, and one-hundred-twenty-seven pounds.

"I trust you had a pleasant trip and found your accommodations acceptable."

"Well, Mr. Purvis, I have always considered travel both a luxury and a privilege." Chess smiled. "There's nothing I like better than meeting new people and visiting new places."

The men seated themselves, Chess sitting in a plush leather armchair across from Melvin's huge oak desk. Melvin lit a Cuban cigar and offered one to Chess, who politely declined. Melvin had a thick accent and greatly enjoyed the genteel lifestyle in which he was born and raised.

"We can dispense with the formalities, Chess," Melvin replied. "We'll be keeping close contact from here on in. You're going to be the Special Agent in Charge on a top secret assignment we've been handed by US Army Intelligence. I'll be the only one you'll report to, and, in essence, you'll be working on the field on your own without any support or backup."

"Sounds interesting," Chess replied mildly as Melvin

pushed a dossier across the desk to him. "What'll be going on about me picking up my check?"

"We'll make an arrangement with your bank so that the check can be mailed directly and deposited without an endorsement," Melvin replied. "Take a look at the pictures in that file, see if there's anyone you recognize."

Chess opened the file and took a glance at the large black-and-white photos. "Well, looks like names in the news. Three in the can and one six feet under."

"That's where the story starts," Melvin revealed. "Fred Barker, killed in an FBI raid with Ma Barker in a shootout at Lake Weir in Florida. Or so the country thinks."

"What does that mean?" Chess wondered.

"Let's turn the clock back a few months before then," Melvin explained. "Alvin Karpis was the Phantom of the Ozarks. Nobody even knew the gang existed before the Hamm kidnapping, and the Barkers didn't make front pages until Ma and Fred got shot up in Florida. Yet it was Karpis who was the mastermind behind the gang, even though the Bureau claimed it was Ma to justify shooting the old lady to pieces. We all know the Boss nailed Karpis, but even that slipped past the public eye."

"Come to think of it, I can't think of much about Karpis that sticks out," Chess admitted.

"You probably never will," Melvin replied. "Everything we got on him is classified, and most of it's witness accounts. They sweated him for three days with no sleep after he got caught, and he wouldn't even give them his parents' address. He had his fingertips surgically whittled down a couple of years ago, so we don't even have his fingerprints."

"So did he find a way to bring Fred Barker back from the dead?"

"No, we did. They were best friends throughout most of their careers, and Fred always did his best to hold his position as the ramrod of the gang. He was always looking for the big score to match what Karpis was bringing in, and one day he thought he came across it. There was a German nobleman, Count Von Rechtschaffen, who was here as a diplomatic envoy during the summer of '34.

He figured if they kidnapped him, they could demand a ransom from our government and the Nazis. Only the count disappeared shortly before the massacre at Lake Weir, and that's where our story begins."

"Let me guess, Barker snatched the count before he got a chance to tell Karpis."

"Not quite. The question was what Barker found out before Lake Weir. We found out the count was acting as the point man for a covert team being sent from Germany to the USA. Military Intelligence was given a report from the British and the French that they did not like. After the count disappeared, their only lead was Barker. When our agents stormed the lake house in Florida, they found Barker hanging on by a thread. They saved his life and sent him to a top-secret military base in New Mexico for questioning. He won't give them a thing because he knows they'll never let him go. He's still out there, and it's part of the reason why we're sending you to make a deal with Karpis."

"Me?" Chess was startled. "Why? I've been involved with a shootout or two, and I've sat in on a few investigations, but I'm not sure I'm up to turning over Public Enemy Number One."

"Everything you'll need is in that file," Melvin assured him. "All you need to know about Karpis, the history and objectives of this mission, all the questions, rebuttals and overcomes are right there. I think you'll be able to make him an offer he can't refuse. This is your time, Chess. You make this happen and there'll be something big at the end of the line for you. The director's got an elephant's memory. Take it from someone who knows. He doesn't forgive and he never forgets. Make it work for you."

莫ヌ莫

Chess was driven to Chicago's O'Hare Airport that afternoon. He caught a flight to Los Angeles International Airport. From there he took a shuttle flight to San Francisco and was driven to the ferry station for the boat ride to Alcatraz Island. It was the most feared prison in American history and was considered escape-proof. It was protected by an elite detachment of armed guards, and maximum security was enforced 24/7. Chess went through numerous checkpoints and his weapon was confiscated. After nearly an hour of processing, Alvin Karpis was brought to a private office in the administration facility.

"Sorry it's taking so long, Mr. Power." The captain of the guard stared at his watch as he impatiently waited for his men to produce Karpis. "Son of a bitch has been in solitary confinement half the time he's been here. He don't take orders from no one, and what's worse, the other cons look up to him. He's like their role model. They figure if Karpis can take whatever we throw at him, then so can they."

"Solitary in a place like this?" Chess marveled. "How does he do it?"

"Funny somebody with your name would ask." The captain chuckled wryly. "He plays chess. My guys sneak down there after hours and play him. He does that memorization crud, playing without a board. Nobody can beat his skinny ass. Rest of the time he sits down there and studies physics, all the latest Einstein stuff. I'm starting to think that he goes into solitary on purpose to load up that superbrain of his."

"Open up the office room!" they could hear the command be given from outside.

At once the door was opened, and a tall, slender man shackled by both wrists and ankles was ushered in. He gave Chess a withering look that would haunt him in his sleep, introducing him to the man known throughout the

American underworld as Old Creepy. Karpis was as tall as Chess but weighed about as much as Little Mel, as he was called. He had a twenty-seven-inch waist, about as slender as most of the women Chess knew. He had light blond hair and was a handsome man with blue eyes, a shapely nose and bow lips.

It was only the frightening stare that made him appear as a cold-blooded psychopath.

"All right, Karpis, you know the drill," the captain barked at him as he sat at the small metal table fastened to the concrete floor. "No physical contact, and you are forbidden to leave your seat. We can and will end this interview at any time, and any violation of the rules will result in further disciplinary action against you. We will also be monitoring this conversation at all times."

"Fellow, you do that and you're likely to have the Federal Government coming down on this prison," Chess admonished him.

"He ain't supposed to know that," the captain huffed. "Open the door!"

Karpis dropped his manacled hands on the table. "So what the hell you want?"

"Well, that's not exactly the greeting I expected from Superbrain," Chess chided him.

"You think I'm gonna go around advertising it, like some sombitch carrying an FBI badge? What you see is what you get, and I decide exactly what you see."

"Looks like we're getting off on the right foot here."

Chess managed a chuckle. "So how do you like this place?"

"I've seen worse."

"Ever plan on getting out?"

"I'm definitely getting out, one way or the other, and it won't be toes up."

"Suppose I told you I could get you and a couple of your friends out of here?"

"Yeah, you and what army?" Karpis scoffed.

"The United States Army," Chess revealed. "There's a top secret mission they've asked the Bureau to undertake. I've been placed in charge of the field operation, and the director has asked that I make a proposal on his behalf. He wants you and a couple of your ex-associates to undertake this assignment in exchange for your early release from prison."

"Nothing doing," Karpis snapped. "That coward made his rep off me. He told the world he personally pinched me. What he didn't tell them that four guys already nailed me, with one holding a tommy gun in my face before he came out of his hiding spot. You think I'm gonna go on a secret mission and let him take the credit?"

"You know, they're planning to keep you in this place for the rest of your natural life. I know you're trying to prove to every con in this prison that even the Rock isn't big enough to crush you. Let's try this on for size: what about your friends? Are you gonna let them rot in here just because of your pride? What kind of rep will you have if this ever got out? Or even worse, are you gonna be able to live with the knowledge that prison life did them in, and you didn't do a thing to help?"

"Knock it off, smart guy," Karpis scowled. "Which friends are you talking about anyway?"

"Doc Barker and Harry Campbell. If you make this deal, we let them out right along with you. Of course, if they compromise the mission, you'll be held responsible. In other words, if one of them decides to hightail it back to Kansas while you're on assignment, all three of you are coming back here to serve the remainder of your sentences. And don't be surprised if they decide to nail a few more years on your tails for good measure."

"Yeah, so who do we have to snatch? Or do you want us to knock off a bank?"Karpis smirked.

"We might need you to knock off a couple of guys for us. Axis saboteurs."

"Axis saboteurs? You mean like Nazi spies?"

"The Germans may not be the only ones involved in this. Everybody knows the Nazis have been serenading the Russians since Stalin rose to power. He's a real big Hitler fan. The theory is if the Nazis ever decide to invade Poland, the Russians'll come right in through the back door and divide the spoil with them. Plus we know the Italians are in bed right alongside them. Now, the three of them know that if they manage to overcome the French and the English, the only thing that'll keep them from taking over the whole world is the USA. If they can find a way to break our spirit and our resolve, they may be able to keep us on the sidelines long enough to take over Europe."

"So it could be a hit squad sent by one of the three, or all three," Karpis mused.

"We're not thinking hit squad, we're thinking saboteurs," Chess corrected him.

"That's because you're dumb, the whole bunch of you," Karpis sneered. "If I blow up your house, if you got any balls you come after me. If I kill your dad, your brother or your best friend, I may have ripped enough of your heart out so you don't have anything left to come back with."

"Well, they say it takes a thief to catch a thief." Chess shrugged. "I guess the same holds true for killers."

"I never knocked off anyone in my life," Karpis growled. "I just know plenty of guys who did."

"Well, no offense, fellow. Let's just say the director thinks that a criminal mind may be best understood by the criminal mind."

"So is that how that pug-faced sombitch caught me, because he's a crook at heart?"

"Suppose I told you I was reporting directly to Deputy Director Purvis. Would that lessen any of that animosity toward us? I'm not sure we'd be able to work at full efficiency if that kind of attitude was polarizing us."

"Who, Purvis, that runt?" Karpis shook his head. "He sent an army in front of him to take Dillinger, same thing with Nelson and Floyd. He's not much better than his boss, but yeah, I could stand him better than old Dogface. Plus, if you're gonna be the guy fronting the show, I suppose I could tolerate you as far as I can see so far."

"Here's what I'm gonna do," Chess disclosed. "I'm gonna let you talk this over with Barker and Campbell. If you can get them to go along with us, I'm pretty sure we can have you out of here by the end of the week. We'll be taking the three you to Fort Sam Houston for briefing, then if things pan out, the operation will begin."

"Fort Sam? That's a military base."

"Technically this is a military operation. Army Intelligence has compiled the information that's been provided to us. They gave the Bureau the assignment but it's their baby. They'll be monitoring our progress every step of the way. Frankly, this country's never been involved with anything like this. Secret agents, saboteurs, espionage—it's not the American way of doing things but sometimes you've gotta fight fire with fire."

"Yeah, well, I think I can speak for all of us when I say we're in," Karpis nodded. "And we'll be bringing hell along with us."

Chess knew deep down that someone would have the Devil to pay.

ღღღ

Alvin Karpis had no reason to trust the government

and never would. He remembered being released from the night and fog of FBI Headquarters after three days of sleep deprivation, enough water to keep him alive, and enough bread to keep him awake.

He gave them nothing, and it was only after the third day and stern medical admonitions that they decided they would end up killing him before he gave them anything. He was sent to the Ramsey County Jail in St. Paul, Minnesota, where he would stand trial for the kidnapping of millionaire beer baron William Hamm and banker Edward Bremer. He would also face charges for the murder of Sheriff C.R. Kellcy of West Plains, Missouri, as well as multiple bank robberies and a great multitude of other crimes.

He marveled in contempt of political editorials deriding the Nazi system of justice, how they were condemned for arresting people without warrants, failing to bring them before a magistrate, and keeping them in jail indefinitely while subjecting them to torture in coercing false confessions. He saw no difference in what this government was doing and what the Nazis were up to. He remembered the torture of Dillinger's girlfriend, Billie Frechette, and the imprisonment of Baby Face Nelson and Machine Gun Kelly's wives for no reason other than to satisfy J. Edgar Hoover's thirst for revenge. He remembered meeting with his court-appointed lawyer who had sold him down the river before they had even met.

"These are great and terrible crimes you've committed, Mr. Karpis." The lawyer, a balding, slender man with curly hair, wire-rimmed glasses, a huge nose and lips, leafed through the thick dossier sitting on the wooden table between him and Karpis in the dark, mildewed cell. "The director—and, in fact, the entire nation—would rather that you come clean and confess your sins before the court and the whole world. If I could go before the judge and jury and plead guilty, guilty, guilty, I believe I could have your sentence reduced from death in the electric chair to life imprisonment without parole."

"Why the hell would I want to do that?" Karpis snapped. "They would have to prove me guilty beyond a shadow of a doubt in a jury trial. I never killed anyone, so that wouldn't stick. Hamm and Bremer could never say they saw me, and none of the kidnap gang would either. As far as any bank robberies, I'm pretty sure that anyone who's ever witnessed one did it with their nose stuck to the ground."

"Mr. Karpis, I'm afraid I would have to strenuously disagree with you." The lawyer's face darkened as he slapped his hands lightly on the desk. "You have left a row of dead bodies in your wake, and there is innocent blood on your hands. Millions of dollars of taxpayers' money have passed through your hands into the pockets of politicians, killers, thieves, and whores across the country. You are Public Enemy Number One, and the director—along with the rest of the country—will not rest until your crimes are paid for in full."

"Hold on." Karpis squinted at him. "You think I've never hired a lawyer before, or appeared in court? You're getting ready to sell me down the river. What are you, one of Hoover's stooges? What happened to my right to fair and qualified representation?"

"Let me assure you, Mr. Karpis—" The man grew defensive. "—I am highly skilled and an expert in my field. I just want there to be no misunderstanding. If I were to make you feel that this would be handled as cavalierly as a traffic ticket, then I would be grossly negligent in my duty. You are on trial for your life, sir, and I would prefer that it be spent in a prison where you could at least indulge in intellectual and spiritual pursuits for the remainder of your natural life. Why on earth would anyone want to see you electrocuted? Certainly it would not be the humanitarian way of doing things, and most definitely not the American way. Why, we don't live in a country surrounded by barbed wire. I believe everyone involved would be much better off if you chose to repent of your crimes and be given a far more civilized punishment."

"So if you don't think it's civilized, then why don't you defend my constitutional right of protection from cruel and unusual punishment?" Karpis taunted him. "Where'd you get your license from anyway, a Sears catalog?"

"I beg your pardon, sir!" The lawyer was indignant. "I'll have you know I have a degree from Harvard, one of the finest universities in the land!"

"Yeah, and in this economy, you think they'd throw you out no matter how dumb you were, as long as your folks could foot the bill?"

"This is an outrage!"

"You got that right. You people got your nerve, riding the Nazis for violating people's civil rights when you're doing the same damned thing here. You guys are nothing but a bunch of fascists yourselves."

"I take that as a personal insult, sir. I am a Jew!"

"Then you should be as concerned about protecting other people's rights as protecting your own. Once they find out how easy it is to grease the skids for criminals, next they go after political opponents and religious objectors. You can't be so stupid not to know that."

"I'll do what I can for you, Mr. Karpis." The man gathered his papers before taking his leave. "It is best to repent and throw yourself at the mercy of the court. However, if you insist on gambling for your life, I will defend you as best I can."

And so Alvin Karpis was eventually sentenced to life imprisonment on Alcatraz Island.

એડ્ડ

When he was first thrown into solitary confinement, Karpis merely laughed. J. Edgar Hoover had obviously been authorized to perform top secret experiments on prisoners after capturing Karpis. It took him a while to figure out, but there had been no other logical explanation for what had happened after his arrest. Hoover ordered the murders of John Dillinger and Baby Face Nelson, and decided to keep Karpis alive for experimentation. Karpis was familiar with Einstein's theory of the time-space continuum. It resonated with concepts Karpis had dwelled on during his incarceration as a juvenile delinquent in Kansas. Time and space coexisted in an ellipsis that coincided with the life span of every individual that ever lived, from Adam and Eve to the last man standing after the Battle of Armageddon. Every life was like a tiny bubble that popped loose from a giant bubble, and when the life was over, it was restored to the giant bubble once more. Crackpots who studied transcendental meditation learned how to move around in the bubble.

They could journey back into the past, and some could even slip into the future. That kind of knowledge was priceless, and Karpis figured that they were using him as a guinea pig to attain that knowledge. The experiment started when he was taken to the downtown Federal Building in St. Paul, Minnesota and chained to a radiator. He would remain there for four and a half days, interrogated around the clock by a never-ending procession of hard-nosed FBI inquisitors.

He found out later that, after twenty-four hours, his brain switched gears from its temporal lobe to the parietal lobe in dealing with the symptoms of blackout. Strangely enough, it enhanced his short-term memory though seriously impairing his long-term capacity. This resulted in the knuckle-draggers thinking that his snappy remarks and repartee indicated he was still lucid, and the experiment went on far longer than it should have as a result. Doctors would later point out that the experiment could have easily resulted in permanent brain damage.

After thirty-six hours, Karpis realized that they must have been spiking his water to make him talk. He was not a drinker, and the few times he had indulged remained vivid in his memory. His speech became slurred, and his reflexes slowed as if he had been placed underwater. He was still giving them smart answers, but it got exceedingly difficult as their voices became garbled. There appeared to be lapses in the dialogue, and he hoped to steer them off-course by discussing Einstein's Theory of Relativity. That seemed to irritate them to no end, and they began threatening him with violence. One agent told him how he had broken two phone books over Doc Barker's head. Karpis figured that the blows would probably get him sent to hospital, and began discussing Einstein more than ever.

At one point he nodded out and was subjected to the usual prods and slaps, but he felt himself slipping into a vortex over which he had no control. He began experiencing vertigo, and felt his testicles shriveling up as his feet no longer touched the ground. He was whirling and spinning, and felt himself being in Kansas for one minute.

All of a sudden the tornado ceased, and he realized he wasn't in Kansas anymore.

He looked around and realized it was nighttime, but somehow they had unchained him from the radiator in the small room and moved him outside to a wooden arm-chair. It was like an electric chair, and his whole body was strapped in an erect position so he was unable to move. He tried to turn his head but it was secured so well that he could barely shift his vision to either side. When he looked ahead, he could see the barren field where they had left him. It appeared to be somewhere on a military base they had used for bombing drills.

The entire landscape was covered with craters, as if they had been hammered since the beginning of time. It appeared to be an unused target area as there were no re-cent sins of activity. There were no signs of fresh dirt, or of erosion. There were only these enormous pits as far as the eye could see.

At length he was able to maneuver his head to the right, and the sight nearly caused his blood to freeze. Over the horizon he could see the stars as if they were close enough to touch. They were speckled like iridescent paint around the sun, glaring as an incandescent sphere dominating the blackness of space. To its left, bigger than anything else besides the sun, was what he knew was the planet Earth. He recognized it from the globes he had seen in school back before he realized he was smarter than his teachers and stopped going. Suddenly it occurred to him that the Government had somehow transported him to the moon.

Just as this occurred to him, he could feel himself prodded and slapped by invisible hands. He realized that the agents had been sent along with him, but the government had seemingly developed some kind of cloaking device so he could not see them. He tried to curse them out but it was as if he was underwater. He was somehow able to breathe, but it was as if he was locked in a closet that was running out of air. His voice traveled to his ears as if trapped in a conch shell, and at long last he drifted back into the vortex.

Life seemed exhilarating in the vortex, and he had lost his fear of falling. It was if he had been returned to his mother's womb and she had total control of her body. She would decide whether he would drop out and get born or not, and she had no intentions of releasing him to the FBI. He snuggled up in his fetal position and began drifting off to hyperspace, the fourth dimension where, Einstein explained, we existed all at once, from beginning to end, life to death, with no definition of time distinguishing one moment from the next. His life was one ultimate event where he experienced every moment, smelled every smell, tasted every taste all at the same time. It was absolutely restful, not having to distinguish one thing from another, nothing to make him feel a dissonance between anything.

Only, Hoover had sent his little FBI astronauts after

him, into his mother's belly, and they began slapping and pinching him again. He got pissed off about that and began to curse them out, but he found that the atmosphere in his mother's womb was the same as that on the moon. He was talking across the continuum, across space and time, and his voice blurred out like that of a record as the phonograph lost power and slowed to a halt. He decided to get up out his place of rest and kick the damned Feds out of his mother's womb. Damned Hoovers didn't respect shit, not even someone's mother's hole.

Whatever he did must have caused his mother to miscarry, and at once he began falling down her passage back into the vortex. Here he regained the sense of vertigo and the fear of falling, and he tumbled helplessly into a bottomless pit where no doctor or midwife awaited to catch him or slap his ass. He tried to scream but they still had his 78 RPM voice set at 33 RPM, and his voice quavered like a sonic bubble as it floated into space like a word balloon in a comic strip that somehow escaped the page and drifted away.

Suddenly he was in a chamber of light back on the moon, and a man in shining white robes appeared before him. He had carefully coiffured hair and bedroom eyes, and there appeared to be blood leaking from the back of his head onto his shoulders. Karpis managed to understand what he was saying as they stood in this underwater atmosphere. He said he was Mr. Kennedy and he had been President of the United States until someone shot him in the head. "We can put you anywhere we want," he explained in an accent which reminded Karpis of his early childhood in Canada. "I was trying to take out this terrorist in Cuba who had taken control of the entire island. I didn't get the job done, so I tried to take out another group that had done the same thing in Vietnam. The Government didn't like the idea and had me shot. I don't like not seeing projects through. Would you be willing to take out this terrorist for me?"

"Cuba?" Karpis squinted at him. "I was just in Cuba a few months ago, everything's fine down there."

"In about twenty years from now it won't be. Terrorists will overthrow the Cuban government and kick your Mafia friends out. I can send you there to take out the terrorist leader. I think you're starting to understand how we can do this."

"I'm not in the killing business. Too bad your flunkies in the FBI are, because you probably could've got the Barkers to do the job for you."

"Yeah, that Hoover's a nasty bastard. He and my brother Bobby have gone round and round a few times. Well, how about taking out the fellow who shot me? Right in front of my wife, in broad daylight during a parade, can you imagine?"

"Sounds like Hoover was asleep at the switch, huh?" Karpis smirked. "Well, like I said, I don't do assassinations. No dice."

"How about Hitler? Would you take out Hitler?"

"Read my lips, buddy. Do you not hear what I just said?"

"How about the Triad? I know you'll go after the Triad."

"Triad? What Triad? What'd I just say?"

"I know you'll take this one. Just wait and see."

"Don't hold your breath," Karpis scoffed, and at once Mr. Kennedy disappeared in a flash of light. He was blinded by the pulsar, and suddenly he was catapulted back into the vortex.

The vertigo hit him again, and he tried clawing his way to something solid. At length the invisible astronauts grabbed his arms again, and he found himself sitting on a cot in St. Paul, surrounded by FBI agents and smelling of sweat and urine.

"Okay, Karpis," Agent Stein, the clown who was running this circus, growled. "You're going before a commissioner in the morning. Mr. Hoover wants us to clean you up."

"Why doesn't he do it himself?" Karpis sneered. "Unless he's gonna show up after it's all over, like last time."

With that, they gave him some coffee, let him take a shower, and allowed him to sleep after four and a half days in hyperspace. Less than a month later, he was sent to Alcatraz Island where he was told he would be spending the rest of his life. He doubted that very much. He was pretty sure they were going to dress him up like some space monkey and launch him back into hyperspace sometime in what human beings would consider the near future.

CHAPTER 2

Campbell had been leading a genteel life after the gang had scored heavily on a train robbery in Garrettsville, Ohio three years ago. The Barkers would have had choice words for him after choosing to settle down in the same state where they had made such a score. Only Campbell met his future wife Gertrude, and suddenly there was more to life than taking big scores with the Karpis-Barker Gang. Gertrude was a wholesome girl who the FBI claimed had been working as a call girl for Claire McGraw. Campbell didn't care about that one way or the other. Times were hard, after all.

He had been called the Limping Man in the Karpis-Barker Gang, as people could never accurately describe him though he was bigger than most of the guys in the crew. He had one of those nondescript faces that one found in cities like Oil City and McClintockville in Pennsylvania where he was born and raised. He had a broad face with wide-set eyes and the clear skin of an Irish maid. Matter of fact, he could have thrown on a baggy dress, a wig and a scarf, and escaped down any street unnoticed as one of the big-boned women from Anywhere, USA. He couldn't truly remember where he got the limp from, and after the government went inside his head and began tinkering around, it was harder than ever. Every time someone asked, he had a different story. Finally people got tired of asking, which was fine by him.

His dad was an oil inspector who started a family in the appropriately named Oil City. They moved to McClintockville and spent thirteen years there before lighting a shuck and heading to Oklahoma. His brother moved up to Casper, Wyoming, and Campbell followed him up there. He got married and had a daughter, but decided he wasn't going to spend the rest of his life as a roughneck.

He took off for Pampa, Texas, and started meeting some hardcases. Alvin Karpis happened to be one of them. Karpis was full of ideas, even back then, and he was so damn smart that Campbell figured they'd never get caught. You couldn't beat the government, though, not with all the scientific technology they had. He had no way of knowing they could search for you with the aid of flying saucers, or pick inside your brain.

The gang split up after the score in Garrettsville, and Campbell wandered down to Bowling Green where he met Gertrude. He brought magic to her life with all that money, and after they got married he had a trailer home set up on her mother's property. He went out and made connections all over town, including a man from Lucas County named Jim O'Reilly. Campbell was introducing himself as Bob Brown, and he and O'Reilly became drinking buddies. He even turned Campbell on to a puppy that he ended up buying for Gertrude. It turned out that O'Reilly was the County Sheriff, but he didn't have a clue who Harry was. That added spice to the relationship, and it constantly affirmed the fact that Campbell had finally escaped his past.

After the fact, he always considered all that highfalutin stuff Karpis always chewed on, that malarkey about the fourth dimension and some space-time continuum or whatever. Apparently, the FBI had one of those flying saucers that the government announced had invaded Earth last year. They put out an alert on the radio, but then called it off and said it had been a test of the emergency broadcast system by somebody called H.G. Wells. That was pretty dumb because now everybody knew they had flying saucers, even though they denied it. Harry knew it for a fact because that was the only way they could have caught him.

J. Edgar Hoover himself showed up, and he was pretty proud of himself. Harry and Gertrude had moved to

Toledo, but by now the flying saucers had locked in on him and there was no place on Earth where he could have escaped to. They showed up at the apartment at five in the morning, and Campbell made little fuss even though Gertrude was totally distracted. She insisted that they were Bob and Gertrude Miller and that they had the wrong man. When they started talking about Alvin Karpis, she figured that must have been another one of those people who had come off the space ships.

Hoover wanted to have O'Reilly fired, but Bob told him to blow it out his ass. He was pretty ticked off about Harry having pulled the wool over his eyes, nonetheless. Everyone but Gertrude was glad when the FBI took Campbell away to Cleveland. Campbell was disappointed that they did not take him in a flying saucer. The FBI guys were glad to get away from Hoover and decided to stop off for a round of golf at a luxurious country club. They asked Campbell if he would like to have one last sip of freedom on them, and he thought that was fine.

In order to throw off the press, they dressed him up as an Irish maid with a bonnet, a big dress, an apron, and work boots. Just in case he decided to run off, they fitted him with a ball and chain. They played eighteen holes just after dawn on a lovely day. Campbell didn't do badly, though he had never played before and was chained to a fifty-pound ball. The club members who inquired were politely told that the big woman was en route to Hollywood to work as a maid for a foreign actress whose name had to be kept secret. The woman had to be kept on a chain because her immigration papers had not been approved yet.

When they got to St. Paul, Campbell got lost in courtroom traffic a number of times because no one knew who he was. A few times he could have walked right out, but he didn't bother because he knew the flying saucer would pick him right up again. Plus, the radio show said they had these disintegrator rays, and he wasn't going to fool with that.

By the time he was supposed to appear for sentencing, he had gotten lost so many times that the judge was entirely distracted. He slammed his gavel on the bench and said that, since Campbell kidnapped Edward Bremer and made so much money from it, he was going to jail for the rest of his life. They sent him off to Alcatraz Island, and he didn't know what he was going to do there for the rest of his life.

All he could do was bide his time until, finally, the military intelligence people arrived and took him to Fort Sam Houston in San Antonio, Texas. It was done in the middle of the night, and once again Campbell was upset because he didn't get a ride in the flying saucer.

Apparently, Fred and Doc Barker did, because everyone thought they were dead but they obviously weren't. Campbell was grateful to the government for letting them out of prison, but he was still skeptical about it all. The government never gave folks something for nothing.

လ.ာ.ာ

The lovely waitress sashayed by booth number four, delighted to serve the meticulously dressed gentlemen who had arrived for the dinner menu. She was quick to take their order and was greatly pleased that the guests had ordered the most expensive steak and seafood entrees on the menu, along with two magnums of vintage champagne. She knew there was going to be a big tip at the end of their visit, and she was going to go out of her way to make this a wonderful dining experience at the renowned Savoy Grill in downtown Kansas City.

Alvin Karpis had lived in a world of paranoia ever since he was sentenced to ten years at the reformatory in Kansas at the age of nineteen. He'd learned to watch over his shoulder, never let his guard down, talk his way out of jams when he could, and use anything he could get his hands on when they called his bluff. He had Lawrence De Vol watching his back until they got arrested in Kansas City and, upon being transferred to the penitentiary in Lansing, he met Fred Barker. Having Fred Barker standing behind you was the best insurance one could have, yet Alvin Karpis would forever sleep with one eye open just the same.

"So where'd you stash all that loot, Ray?" Fred grunted as he lit a Cuban cigar. "The rest of us got cleaned out like a cuckoo clock. Where'd you stick all that cash so the Hoovers didn't find it?"

Karpis, Doc, and Campbell had gotten the shock of their lives upon arriving at Fort Sam Houston a few days ago and waiting in a room until Fred was brought in to greet them. Fred, who was nearly killed at Lake Weir, was kept alive just as Melvin Purvis had told Chess Power. He had been locked up in maximum security by the US Army and reported dead by the FBI. Operation Spycatcher had been in the works since the Allies learned of the Axis plot, and Barker had been kept under wraps until the mission could be initiated.

"What're you planning to do, stink up the place before I can shove a fork in my mouth?" Karpis growled, ignoring Fred's question.

All four men were wearing $100 silk suits, along with Panama and straw boater hats which they checked at the door. Karpis had gotten in touch with his Mob connections, with whom he had left a sizeable amount of cash for safekeeping. He had salted away large sums from various bank robbery scores with numerous underworld sources and could draw upon them at short notice by request.

"C'mon, Ray, I haven't had a decent cigar since before we got blasted at Lake Weir," Fred whined, "especially Cuban."

"Well, why don't you go outside and smoke the damn thing," Karpis growled.

"The hell I will." Fred, who stood five feet, four inches and weighed 120 pounds, was about as big as

Melvin Purvis. He had the lifeless stare of a shark and was just as coldblooded a killer. "Suppose it's raining?"

"Okay, then," Karpis replied. "Doc, why don't you go outside and see if it's raining?"

"Right," Doc replied, rising from his chair. He was the same height and weight as his brother, though his hair was black and Fred's was dark blond.

"C'mon, Doc, he's just funnin' with you," Campbell said. He stood five feet, seven inches and weighed 135 pounds, his brown hair and eyes and placid composure giving him the least menacing appearance of the four. "Hey, the girl's bringing the appetizers. Maybe you can blow the smoke sideways, eh, Freddie?"

"You guys are real pains in the ass, y'know?" Fred grumbled, snuffing the cigar out in an ashtray.

"At least they're not sendin' you out to see if it's rainin' when it ain't," Doc replied.

Arthur "Doc" Barker was the personification of the Ozark hillbilly, a man who appeared to have never read a book or entertained one lofty thought in his life. Yet he was deadly when crossed and would draw a gun on a man who he perceived was belittling him. Plus, he had Fred standing behind him as well, and Fred would never tolerate anyone disrespecting his older brother. Fred, it was known, would kill a man just as soon as look at him. Between the two of them, Karpis had two of the deadliest gunmen in the USA watching his back, and the law and the underworld were well aware of the fact.

Karpis had made several calls once they had been released from Fort Sam and driven to San Antonio International Airport. They'd arrived in Kansas City just last night and Karpis called his most trusted connections, swearing them to secrecy that he was back in circulation. He had lots of underworld guys with an ear to the ground, looking for German visitors, diplomats, and immigrants in the area, as well as any Russians.

It would be harder to finger the Italians, but he was fairly certain that the Mafia would sort out its own laundry.

He was trying to figure out how they could score while they were out on the streets without the feds catching on. If they went sideways on this deal, there was a good chance the feds would rub them out for the double-cross. This would have to be his masterpiece, but he had to plan it carefully and keep it to himself until he was ready. If the others knew what he was planning, they just might take the initiative and get something going before he could stop them...if he even could.

"Say, doll face, what do you think about you and me checking out the Plaza this weekend?" Fred turned on the charm as the waitress set their calamari and pasta appetizers before them. "I've got a place right by there, we can take a stroll and see what's cooking."

"Well, I don't know if I'm working this weekend," she replied, though she ended up giving him her phone number and walking away with stars in her eyes. Guys with that kind of money during this Depression were hard to come by.

"Okay, Romeo, where are you gonna come up with that kind of dough?" Karpis narrowed his eyes as he took a bite of calamari. "and what makes you think you'll be in town long enough to do anything with it?"

"Hey, look," Fred said flatly, "don't tell me you're going along with that flatfoot program. They just sprung the four top guys from our gang. We hightail it outta here, we can go down to Arkansas, round up a new bunch of yeggs and start fresh. They'll never catch us this time."

"You want to trust a new bunch of bank robbers? C'mon, Fred, think it over," Karpis insisted. "They just cut us in on a top-secret operation. If you go sideways, they'll be sure that you spilled the beans somewhere. They'll blow us away in a heartbeat. If we do this job and bump these assassins off, we can reappear somewhere and start fresh without having the US Army on the look-out for us."

"Yeah, you never know." Doc frowned. "With all this talk about war going on, we just might end up getting drafted."

"You know—" Karpis glared at him, but relented as Fred gave him a pleading look.

"Say, excuse me, fellows." A man approached their table. "I just couldn't help myself. I don't mean to be presumptuous, but I just had to ask. Did anyone ever mention that you look just like Alvin Karpis?"

"No, why? Who's that?" Karpis quickly shot his fingers into his lapel pocket and produced a pair of gold-rimmed glasses, slipping them on. At once he took on the semblance of a college professor, to the surprise of both the inquirer and his friends.

The man smiled. "Public Enemy Number One. He's doing life in Alcatraz. No offense, friend. Obviously, you're not that type. It's just a remarkable resemblance. My mother followed the FBI's War on Crime religiously over the years, and she had so many Karpis pics around the house, you'd think she worked for J. Edgar Hoover."

"Well, I don't know how you could've missed the fact that he looks just like Freddie Barker." Doc pointed at his brother as Campbell cupped his forehead in disbelief.

"I gotta go to the can," Fred grunted as he rose from his seat.

No one but Karpis noticed that he nudged his brother in the back of the head with an elbow in passing.

"Hey, at least it's over. You don't have to watch the street when you're waiting in line at the bank anymore." The man smiled as he walked away. "Have a good night, fellas."

It was the kind of thing Karpis's new nightmares were made of. Even though the feds had let him walk free, there was still the police and sheriffs in the podunk towns who would easily think that Public Enemy Number One had escaped without anyone even knowing. He knew that the kind of people who played cops and robbers were the same kind of people on both sides of the fence. There were Doc Barkers in uniform all over the country, the type who would shoot first and ask questions later.

There was no way of knowing that the fellow who had smiled and walked away was not running for a phone booth, hoping his name would be mentioned in the newspaper article announcing that Alvin Karpis had been recaptured.

About two tables away, another customer had not blown the incident off quite as cavalierly as Karpis had hoped. Cat the Bounty Hunter was a legend throughout the Midwest, having brought in some of the most wanted criminals in the region's history. Bob Feta was a two-time loser, a cat burglar who began using his skills to capture fugitives using false identities to sequester themselves in high-rise luxury apartments. At six foot, 210 pounds, he had the size and fighting skills to take out the criminals he hunted down.

He knew Karpis, Campbell, and Doc were in Alcatraz and Fred was six feet under, but these fellows were dead ringers and they had to be playing an angle somewhere.

He also knew that the Boss of Bosses, Lucky Luciano, was under indictment for white slavery in New York. This meant that a major power struggle was brewing between the Five Families that would affect every other Mafia Family in the country. It was well-known that the Mob had sanctioned all the bandit gangs across the nation, in order to escape the heat from the FBI's flying squads. Putting together a hit team composed of gangster lookalikes would be an ideal way to rub out a Boss, a way everyone would think of as an act of retaliation.

He decided that he would tail these guys and find out where they were staying. From there he could do some snooping and get some names and do some checking around. If he came across anything he could get in touch with Tom Pendergast's people at City Hall. Pendergast was the king of the volcano in KC, the political kingpin who had control over everything, from the political domain to the cop-controlled underworld.

Pendergast was the one who would be able to set a price on these guys and decide just how he wanted them served up.

"Say, Ray, you got a thing for that coffee pot?" Campbell asked as Karpis inspected the silver vessel, tilting it from different angles as it sat on a warmer. "Gonna buy one for yourself?"

"Nah, just looking." Karpis studied it carefully. "Now, Doc, don't move your goddamn head. There's a mug sitting around two tables behind me and he's been staring at us for the last fifteen minutes. I've been watching his reflection. I don't know or care if he's a cop or not. We just gotta figure on losing him when we leave here."

"What's up with you mugs?" Fred asked as he rejoined them. "My brother looks like he's gonna put a hole in somebody."

"Ray doesn't want you to look at the guy sitting two tables behind him," Doc faced the table rigidly, his eyes darting everywhere but sideways.

"You want me to take care of it?" Fred's fingers caressed the .38 revolver that Karpis had gotten them from a stash outside Kearney on their way from the airport.

"C'mon, Fred, gimme a break." Karpis set the pot down softly. "Let your girlfriend take care of it."

"What are you, nuts?" Fred demanded. "I haven't even taken her out yet, and you think I'm gonna have her shoot somebody?"

"There's gotta be something in the water in this place." Karpis shook his head in exasperation. "Just call her over, Freddie, okay?"

Fred called the waitress over and she cheerfully came by, walking over to Karpis as instructed. He gave her a $20 along with detailed instructions. She appeared reluctant but was not going to argue against that kind of money.

Bob Feta watched the waitress leave the table and riveted his gaze on Karpis, studying his gestures and mannerisms, wanting to pass on as much information as possible. He saw the man was right-handed, spoke in an even voice, and appeared to be the leader of the group. He was also the one who appeared to be footing the bill and was probably their money man. If Feta could get some information on that man, it would tell him everything about the quartet and where they were going.

"Sir, would you like some—oh my gosh!" the girl gasped as the coffeepot slipped from her grasp and bounced off Feta's table. Feta leaped to his feet, barely dodging the cascade of steaming liquid that spilled onto the carpeted floor. "I'm so sorry!"

"All right, all right!" Feta snapped, stepping away from the table, inspecting his pants to ensure that he hadn't gotten any stains on his suit. "Luckily there's no harm done."

"Oh, sir, I am so sorry," she made a feeble attempt to daub his trousers. "Let me bring you a wet cloth. Are you sure you're okay?"

"Look, I said—" Feta blustered then at once jerked his head to the side. His worst fears were realized as the table of four, just two spaces away, was completely deserted.

છ૭છ૭

Karpis had rented a 1938 Dubonnet Xenia, its innovative front-end suspension and steering making it an excellent getaway car if the need arose. It got them out of the downtown area in a short time, cutting down Highway 78 to the suburbs of Independence.

They pulled over alongside a small tavern where the

Barkers and Campbell ordered beers while Karpis made some more calls.

"Okay, look, here's the deal," Karpis informed them as he returned to the table about a half hour later. "I've arranged a sit down with Pendergast's people tomorrow night. Harry and I'll be meeting with the Chief of Police, Otto Higgins. He's Pendergast's muscle man. He directs traffic around town. We're gonna be looking for an in at the benefit rally at the Hotel Phillips this weekend. They're raising money in support of Senator Truman, they're pushing him hard in the coming elections. From what Power told me, if the Nazis are making any moves here in the Midwest, they're gonna be at that fundraiser, trying to make connections and pick up some inside information."

"Ray, are you losing it?" Fred stared at him. "We're going face to face with the chief of police? The guy's gonna have to be legally blind not to make us."

"Look, first of all, *we* are in Alcatraz, remember?" Karpis explained patiently. "Second of all, the guy's gonna be in a state of denial. The Pendergast organization's catching serious heat right now all over the country, from DC to the governor's office. He'll be more worried about building Truman up for a big run at Washington than looking at us. We're going in like a couple of front guys for the San Antonio Mob. We'll drop some names, make some promises, spread some rumors, and see what happens."

"What San Antonio Mob are you taking about?" Campbell wondered.

Karpis smiled. "The one that Chess Power is the Boss of."

"Holy smoke!" Doc gaped at him. "He's gotta be even smarter than you!"

Fred raised a palm toward Karpis. "Go easy, Ray."

"Okay, listen," Karpis managed to control himself. "Higgins'll make some calls to check our story. After that he won't have a lot of time. I'm gonna tell him we gotta get up close to Truman so we can pitch him on some investments. The con is that we'll be pumping some money up here from Texas, and a chunk of that'll be going into the Pendergast machine to invest in their Truman campaign. If Higgins makes the intro and we can get near Truman, we'll be able to get a good look at any newcomers on the political scene. If these Triad assassins are making a move in this direction, they'll have to be passing where we can see them."

"Ray, you gotta be taking a big chance," Campbell insisted. "First you're going face to face with the chief of police, then you wanna get close to the senator. Don't you think these guys read the papers? Your face was plastered on every front page in the country just a couple of years ago."

"See, Doc? Whatever you got is contagious." Karpis shook his head. "C'mon, Harry. We're in Alcatraz, how many times do I gotta say it? The feds made a deal with the bulls, the story is that we got hauled down to Fort Sam for questioning on that thing with that missing Count Von Rechtschaffen. The warden gave the order that nobody says crap. They're not getting nothing from Alcatraz, even if they bring my mom to the hotel to put the finger on me."

"Your mom's coming all the way out here?" Doc squinted. "I thought you said she don't like to travel."

"Okay, I've had enough." Karpis rolled his eyes. "Finish up and let's get back to the Plaza. I wanna get some shuteye. I got a long day tomorrow. Harry, I want you to go out tomorrow and find out all you can about Truman, where he lives, where he eats, how he breathes. Fred, I'm gonna need you to check out some of those old dives on Troost Avenue and see if we can recruit some help. Make up an alias, tell 'em you're putting together a gang, give them my Grand Avenue phone number."

"What should I do?" Doc asked.

"You go down and case the zoo," Karpis retorted. "Make sure they don't put you back behind bars."

"The zoo?" Doc was incredulous. "What kinda score are we gonna make at the zoo?"

"Hey." Karpis shrugged as Fred and Campbell lowered their heads. "We gotta start somewhere."

"Oh," Doc said contemplatively.

The four partners left the saloon shortly afterward, unaware that they were in for one of the most harrowing episodes of their career.

၄၁၄၁

The gang headed straight for bed when they reached the villa. Karpis slept fitfully and found himself waking in a cold sweat, staring at the ceiling trying to remember where he had last laid his head. It took him a moment to realize he was no longer in the hellhole that was Alcatraz. Waking up on the Rock was a jolt to the system, a jump start that switched one's consciousness into survival mode.

There was always a concern as to whether the guards were coming into the cell for an unannounced search, or if another inmate was searching through your things, or if cockroaches had invaded your cot.

It also took a minute or two to remember if you were back in the Hole, a place where a spot seemed to have been reserved for a problematic prisoner like Karpis.

He got out of bed and decided to step out onto the veranda for a breath of fresh air to clear his head. As he walked into the shadowy living room, he could see a silhouette of a man standing by the window, a machine gun perched on his hip."Whassamatter, couldn't sleep?"

"Nah. Still trying to shake off the jailhouse jitters." Karpis walked past where Fred stood, pulling open the sliding glass door open wide so that the breeze from the creek wafted into the spacious room.

"I know the feeling," Fred replied, taking a deep drag off his Lucky Strike as he gazed down past the creek to the Plaza on the other side. "You can't get rid of the idea that someone's gonna be coming for you. Maybe the feds change their mind, or them Nazi bastards find out we're onto them, or even the Mob decides to rub us out to make sure the cops don't come snooping around. No matter how it comes, you can be damn sure I'm not getting caught unsuspecting."

Karpis knocked a Chesterfield out of the pack and lit up. "We haven't really got to talk since we've been out."

"I know. I haven't had much to say, not even to Doc."

"I'd like to know what happened to Ma."

There was a long silence.

"I've been trying to kick it out of my head, but it keeps sneaking back in."

"That's all right," Karpis blew a stream of smoke toward the marbled floor. "Maybe some other time."

"It was kinda like one of them storms we'd see down in Oklahoma," Fred reflected. "Things were real peaceful, maybe a tad too peaceful. You know, the calm before the storm. Them bastards pulling up in their cars out behind the bushes along the property was like the storm clouds. You see 'em but there's no time to prepare for it. When that tornado starts roaring in, all you can do is run for cover. Only sometimes there's nowhere to hide."

"Yep, those Hoover boys got it down to a science," Karpis agreed. "After Baby Face Nelson took out all those G-Men, they don't move a muscle unless there's a gang of them at the ready. They don't come in pairs any-more."

"By the time I got the Tommies out, they'd already surrounded the house," Fred continued quietly. "I relive that night over and over again in my dreams. If I could do it all over again, I would've gotten Ma out of that house before one shot was fired. I still don't know what I was thinking at the time. Maybe I figured I could hold them off and play for time, hoping something might happen to turn things around. I think it was more about the notion of seeing Ma in handcuffs, being taken to jail. There was no way in hell I could have lived with that."

"None of us could've," Karpis assured him. "Any one of us would have fought like the devil."

"I did, Ray, you can be damn sure I did." Fred's voice grew husky with emotion. "That fight must've gone on for hours. All I could think of was Ma hiding under the kitchen table, scared out of her wits, while them feds were tearing that place apart with every kind of bullet you can think of. I loaded every gun I had in the house and began setting a couple at every window. They thought there was a gang of us up there, but after a while they figured out it was just me and Ma. Hell, I shot the shit out of them cars of theirs, it looked like a used car lot out there, but they had us cornered and they knew we had no way out."

"I'll tell you, Fred, there's not a one of us who wouldn't have gladly been there with you, and surely we would've got killed right alongside you."

"I honestly can't tell you when a bullet hit Ma." Fred wiped a tear from his eye. "I know I got hit once or twice, and I was hurt pretty bad but I kept running from window to window, loading up guns and emptying 'em out at them bushes wherever I could see gunsmoke. Then I took a head shot, and it was game over. Hear tell I was out for weeks, slipped off into a coma. I remember bits and pieces since I was still alive, but I can't honestly say whether I was dreamin' or not. I finally came to in a military hospital where they had me chained to a bed. That's when they told me what happened and gave me the terms and conditions of their deal. I figured anything'd be better than rotting in prison, especially since they told me they were bringing some of you fellows in on it."

"Nobody told us a damned thing until we all got brought together," Karpis revealed. "I remember seeing those pictures of you and Ma in the paper, and I was sick for days, though I didn't let on to no one. Then they staged that prison break and spread the word that Doc got killed. I still think of what dirty sons of bitches they were to have us all think that the three of you were gone when, in reality, Ma was the only one we lost."

"I don't know how long I can live like this, Ray." Fred shook his head. "We've been taking scores since we were biting ankles. Even if we kill them Nazi bastards and they set us free, I don't know how I'm gonna get by. Maybe if they set me up like Frank James or Cole

Younger and have me go around telling folks about my exploits, I might be able to make my way. Otherwise, I just can't see how I'll make my way clear of going out yeggin' again."

"There's always a way around everything." Karpis snuffed his cigarette before walking past Fred and patting his shoulder. "Just give me time, and I'll find it. Go on and get some sleep. I'm sure it'll go lighter now you got that story off your chest."

"Thanks, Ray," Fred replied.

Fred set the machine gun by the doorframe and slowly made his way up to the guest bedroom. To his surprise, he enjoyed the first night of uninterrupted sleep he had since the fatal gun battle with the FBI at Lake Ocala.

CHAPTER 3

Karpis remembered his last days in general population at Alcatraz before they threw him in the Hole for more time than any man before him. His last meal was with Campbell, and they stood in line together as inedible gruel was slopped onto their trays along with a glass of yellow water and moldy bread. They found a table in a far corner of the slowly-filling mess hall, with guards armed with nightsticks walking around looking for someone to bludgeon.

"This place is getting weirder, Ray." Campbell poured salt all over his food to give it some kind of flavor. "There's a whole bunch of guys who don't know what they're here for. They say they just got picked up off the street and tossed in jail, then got sent out here.

They said that they got accused of being enemies of the state."

"Sounds like a lot of malarkey to me." Karpis winced as he took a bite of the rancid food. "You know everybody in this damned place is innocent."

"I think these guys are on the level," Campbell insisted. "Any yegg can tell the difference between a street guy and a civilian. These guys don't have a clue about anything. You'll come across one of 'em soon enough. They walk around like they woke up on another planet."

"I don't know of anyone who didn't think they were in another world when they came to this shithole," Karpis growled, glancing up at the prisoners at nearby tables who stared out sightlessly as men without hope.

"Do you think the Hoover boys might be rounding people out for talking against the government?" Campbell wondered. "After all, they've been carrying on about subversives, saying there's communists and Nazis all over the country trying to bring our nation to its knees. I've always thought that people had a right to speak their minds, and that people could vote whichever way they wanted. Now you know I don't give a damn about politics, and I'd just as soon see them elect the dog catcher for president for all the good it'll do you and me. Still, it just seems kinda fishy that they could throw fellows in here just for having different ideas about politics."

"Yeah, well, I don't give a damn about politics either." Karpis grimaced as he took another bite of hash.

"What I do know is that Keynesian economics I've been reading about stinks of socialism to me. Roosevelt thinks that he's going to increase government spending and manipulate the country's monetary policy to end the recession. He's going down the same road as those damn commies in Russia, any idiot can see that,"

"I don't mean to contradict you or poke fun at you, Ray, but sometimes you talk like you come from another planet. You darn sure don't talk like folks in Kansas."

"Hell, if we got paroled out of this garbage dump, I'd probably start carrying on about this damn socialist administration and the Hoovers'd toss me right back in here."

"Psst!" Campbell warned him as he saw a guard approaching from the corner of his eye. "Here comes one of the screws! Follow my lead!"

Karpis watched in puzzlement as Campbell put his napkin over his mouth and held it there.

"Word is that the government's got a new-fangled device that lets them read your lips when you're talking," Campbell said past his napkin. "If you cover your lips, you got 'em beat."

"That's the dumbest thing I ever heard of," Karpis scoffed, giving the guard a dirty look before holding his own napkin to his lips.

"Everything all right, Karpis?" the guard asked, glowering, as he swaggered by menacingly.

"It was fine until that stench came through the same time you did," Karpis sneered.

With that, the guard called for reinforcements before Karpis was dragged to the warden's office and sentenced to some more hard time in the hole. He would not see Campbell again until the gang reunion at Fort Sam Houston.

಄಄಄

The fundraiser for Senator Harry S. Truman at the Hotel Phillips in downtown Kansas City was one of the biggest social events of the year. All of the biggest and brightest stars on the local scene had been invited, and it was a black tie affair in which everyone came dressed to the max. "Boss Tom" Pendergast had a table at stage left in the grand ballroom, and there was a line of well-wishers waiting to pay tribute to the man who had the City of Fountains in his vest pocket.

One of his top confidants, Otto Higgins, had a table at stage right which entertained a short line of people wanting to make their visits short and sweet. Many of the movers-and-shakers who had other affairs to attend to stopped by and exchanged words with Higgins before money was donated and promises exchanged. Among those in the short line was Ray Cullen and Clark Kent, who finally reached the table where Higgins stood to greet them.

Karpis had gotten away from the others long enough to take a walk along Brush Creek near the Plaza where he had rented a villa for years before his arrest. He breathed the sweet smell of freedom that blended with the aroma of the flowing water, and admired the Canadian geese that flew in for a respite before migrating south. Kansas City was always one of his favorite cities, and he came here to recharge his batteries after particularly trying bank jobs and kidnappings. Plus he had plenty of underworld connections here, and it was never too difficult to make deals or put things together in short order.

He always considered the irony of the overweight shysters in their hundred-dollar suits, driving around in their luxury cars, bilking people out of their life savings during this Depression without a shred of conscience. People said the same thing about gangsters, but Karpis always thought there was a big difference between robbing a bank full of armed guards, and foreclosing on a man's home and putting his family on the street with the stroke of a pen.

People like J. Edgar Hoover and Franklin Roosevelt could pontificate about ending the criminal plague, while standing back and smiling as people were left homeless in the name of free enterprise. Karpis much preferred dishonest politicians like Tom Pendergast, who got all the choice cuts but always left some scraps on the table for the poor souls on the street.

"Mr. Higgins, I'm Ray Cullen and this is my associate, Mr. Kent." Karpis shook hands with Higgins as he introduced himself and Campbell. They both appeared debonair in their black tuxedos, Karpis wearing his gold-rimmed glasses and slicking back his hair.

"My pleasure." Higgins beckoned one of his under-lings to take his place at the table as he walked off to a far corner with his two visitors. "We made a couple of calls to check your references and you do seem to be quite sol-id and in good standing in your community, to say the least. You know, San Antonio and Kansas City have al-ways had strong relations over the decades, from one cat-tle town to another. Hopefully we'll be able to update that relationship and make it even stronger."

"That's exactly what we got in mind," Karpis as-sured him. "Look, our people are seeing yours as a role model, the way of the future. With this Depression going on, the only way the common man can stay afloat is in the underground economy. If the politicians can make it easier for people to cut corners, people can have enough for themselves, and even some left over to pay tribute to their benefactors. We see you doing it here, and we've got our own good ol' boy system that's working back home. This Truman guy, though, he's going places and we wanna go with him. Can you get us in to see him?"

"Truman's not exactly our boy, Ray." Higgins frowned. "He can be as stubborn as one of our Missouri mules at times. Sure, he's in with Boss Tom, but he defi-nitely doesn't take orders. I'm not sure what kind of deal you're gonna be able to make with him. What'd you have in mind, anyway?"

"We heard he's setting up a haberdashery here in the metro," Karpis replied. "We've got some connections with world-renowned tailors in the San Antonio area. Ever hear of Penner's?"

"Not right off-hand," Higgins said slowly, painfully aware of being dressed in his off-the-rack suit at this affair.

"Tell you what, Chief, I'll have a couple of his suits shipped right to your doorstep," Karpis patted him on the shoulder. "We'll have you looking like Clark Gable in no time. Just give me your measurements and your home address. How about hooking me up with Truman in the meantime?"

"Sure thing," Higgins beamed, dutifully writing down both his and Truman's addresses and phone numbers on the back of Pendergast business cards. Karpis thanked him for the information and soon returned with Campbell to their table in the rear where the Barkers awaited.

"Get it done, Ray?" Doc asked as Fred poured them shots of bourbon.

"Yeah, got his address and Truman's," Karpis replied. "After we get done with this job, maybe we'll come back here and kidnap that sombitch. I bet Pendergast'd pay plenty to get him back, for all the information we'd make him cough up."

"So what's our next move?" Campbell asked.

"I'm thinking we'll head back to the condo," Karpis decided. "You guys can go out to the Plaza and pick out some dames for yourselves. "I've got to make some calls, see what I can get on Truman. I'm figuring we can drive by his place after church tomorrow."

"Geez, Ray, I don't wanna go to church," Doc whined.

"I'm not sure God wants you there either," Karpis replied.

Karpis was not a drinker and had a glass of tonic water as he waited for the others to finish up. They were finally ready to leave just as the ballroom began filling up, and Karpis handed the valet a dollar to have the Xenia brought around.

The valet was beaming as he held the doors for the foursome, and they all waved as Karpis hit the gas and sped off.

ꙮꙮꙮ

Four men in a car watched the other four men in the Xenia drive off.

"Okay, so those are the ringers you told us about," the baby-faced man sitting in the driver's seat asked.

"Sure are," Bob Feta replied. "That guy looks just like Alvin Karpis without those glasses."

"So whaddaya wanna do about those guys, Joey?"

Joe Adonis shrugged. "We need to get a make on 'em, Lepke,"

He was one of the New York Mafia's top political fixers, and Louis Buchalter was one of the co-founders of Murder Inc., the Mafia's assassination crew.

"Tell ya one thing, if they got into this party, they got some pretty good connections," Adonis continued. "Whether or not they're good for us is what we gotta find out."

Feta had phoned his own connections in New York and learned that Vito Genovese, one of the founding fathers of the New York Commission, had come to KC along with Adonis and Genovese to do business with the Pendergast Machine. Feta had asked for an audience and met with Adonis that afternoon at the Savoy Hotel. Adonis spoke to his own companions, and now Feta found himself in a car with Adonis, Buchalter and Vito Genovese.

Genovese was one of the major players on the NY crime scene, the head of one of its Five Families. It was said that he was the heir apparent to Charlie "Lucky" Luciano, who had become the target of the United States Attorney's Office in its effort to take down organized crime in New York City. It was widely rumored that Genovese had been instrumental in greasing the skids in having his rival convicted and deported from America, but speaking in public against Don Vitone often led to a death sentence, courtesy of Buchalter. Most of the top

Mob figures were watching and waiting to see how things panned out, but this news from Bob Feta made Genovese wonder if there was someone else wanting Luciano out of the picture.

"Okay, here's the deal," Genovese decided. "I give you a grand to stay on those guys' tails. We know Frank Nitti blackballed all those bank robbers up in Chicago, so maybe they all figured on getting into something more profitable. Obviously they're tight with somebody with muscle, just like Joey said. I wanna know who they're with and what they're driving around for. If you saw 'em at the Savoy, and now they're over here, they've got a pretty good bankroll behind 'em. Good thing you came to us, Feta. If this works out to our benefit, there'll be some more work coming your way. You can count on it."

"Thank you, Don Vitone," Feta groveled before him as he turned sideways in the passenger seat to face his benefactor.

"No problem," Genovese smiled, his craggy grin emphasizing the wrinkles in his football-shaped head. "Look, we'd drop you off somewhere but we're running late."

"That's fine, Mr. Genovese," Feta let himself out, bidding farewell to one and all before disappearing into the night.

"Friggin' bounty hunters," Adonis said disgustedly. "Scum of the earth."

"You get that valet to wipe the slime trail off the seat

before we pick this piece of crap back up," Genovese snorted before Joey steered the car into the valet parking area.

Despite their loathing, they knew that Feta was one of the best in the business, and this Karpis look-alike now had a bloodhound on his tail with the Mob holding his leash.

჻

Campbell and the Barkers hit the Plaza dressed in their finery with a few hundred in their pockets, courtesy of Karpis who had stayed behind to catch up on his homework. As soon as they left Karpis's luxury townhouse overlooking Brush Creek along the Plaza in midtown KC, Karpis got on the phone and called his connections on the Dragnet.

The Dragnet was one of the most sophisticated underground information networks on the planet. It was organized by an association of renegade government workers who exchanged classified information amongst themselves and provided it to subscribers for $10,000 per year. Karpis had never been hesitant to invest in a good deal that would enhance his business opportunities, and this particular one placed a world of knowledge at his fingertips.

According to sources, the American Nazi Party was holding a rally in Madison Square Garden in February of

next year. The goal was to emphasize the racial harmony
between the USA and Germany, as Germans comprised
the second-largest ethnic group in America. It was also
meant to demonstrate political unity against the com-
munist plague that was sweeping the globe. They weren't
about to play the religion card as the Jewish population in
NYC was as large as that of Eastern Europe, up to six
million strong. Regardless, there was no love lost between Karpis and the Axis powers, largely due to his
Lithuanian ancestry.

Although his father was of German descent and his
mother part Irish, they were both born and bred Lithuani-
ans who left their native land over persecution. Karpis
wouldn't have blinked if the Barkers blew a commie's
brains out, and rubbing out a Nazi would have been no
big deal either. Still, he had to keep the boys under control until he could get a grip on who they were after and
why.

From what he was being told, Count Von
Rechtschaffen had been a major fundraiser who was rak-
ing in some big bucks for the Nazis in Hollywood. He'd
disappeared from the scene recently, and it was speculated that he had gotten in trouble with the Nazis in Germany and went into hiding. Apparently, Chess Power
thought he had gone undercover to coordinate the efforts
of this hit squad. Logic dictated that if Karpis found Von
Rechtschaffen, he would find the hit men.

Regardless, Karpis and the boys would be paying a

visit to Harry Truman's home in Independence tomorrow afternoon. If the Nazis had attended the fundraiser as Power suspected, then they would have gotten directions to Truman's house as easily as he had. The only problem he foresaw was either Fred or Doc blowing them away on the spot, in exchange for their Stay Out Of Jail cards. If he could avoid that scenario, then quite possibly the point dogs would lead them to the hunting party. After that, Karpis wouldn't mind picking up a one-way ticket to Canada, or wherever else they might send him to resume his career as the greatest yegg of all time.

He remembered his first night back in civilian life, when they were flown back to Kansas City and given two-night hotel accommodations giving them enough time to find their own way. Karpis had made a few calls and had money made available to him from a local loan shark he had left a sizeable amount of money with. He then decided to take a walk around the midtown area though it was well after midnight. He was concerned that a cop might spot him and take him in, but he was dressed in a suit and tie and would probably not arouse undue suspicion.

"Hey, mister, got a light?"

He found himself confronted by a red-haired girl of average size, with green eyes and a pretty face that was blemished by dark teeth from a lifetime of smoking. She had a nice figure with shapely legs and firm hips, but her bosom was not quite developed.

"Yeah, sure." He pulled his lighter so she was able to spark up her Pall Mall. "Say, isn't it kinda late for you to be out here?"

She took a deep drag. "Well, I couldn't sleep."

"I know what that's like."

They turned and walked in step down the street toward Grand Avenue. He saw three guys standing in a doorway smoking cigarettes and could not figure what they were up to.

Maybe they were counting down time before going on a score, or possibly just hanging out. If he was a cop he would have busted their chops.

It was easy to see how cops were such bastards at this time of night.

"Where are you from?" she asked.

"Canada," he half-ribbed her.

"What part?"

"Montreal."

"I hear it's beautiful there. Is it far from Niagara Falls?"

"A couple of hours' drive. Where are you from?"

"I came up from San Antonio."

"What the hell are you doing up here?"

"I don't know. I hitched a ride with a trucker. I was getting a hard time from the cops back there. I was in a halfway house but I couldn't stand the people. I was trying to find another place to stay but they kept after me when I couldn't find anything. They've got the Salvation

Army bunkhouses and the YWCA, but if you don't get there early enough they get filled up."

"You're not a bad-looking dame. Why don't you find yourself a nice guy?"

"There are no nice guys, at least not on the street. The guys out here are as down on their luck as I am, even worse. If they got a place, they're barely holding onto it. Once they get you in there, they expect you to make up the difference to keep it, and if they can't make the rent they blame you for it. Then they try to get you to go out begging or sell your ass. No thanks."

Karpis shrugged. "Lots of girls are selling their asses these days."

"Yeah? Well, why don't you go sell *your* ass?"

He chuckled. "You got a point there."

What really made him feel bad was knowing that if he gave her money, she'd make a beeline straight to the liquor store or some dope den first thing in the morning, if she could wait that long. Sure she might get herself a room and something to eat, but the money would only be a quick fix until she ran short and ended up on the street again.

He had met too many people like that in his life, lost souls looking for a place to run away from. It was a damn shame because she wasn't a bad looking girl.

A trip to the dentist and a dress shop would make her good as new, but she wouldn't be able to clean up the mess inside her head.

"Hey, you think I can stay with you tonight?"

He winced as he'd known the question was coming.

"I'll take the couch, or sleep in a chair. I'd be gone by morning if you want."

"Nah, can't do it." He shook his head. "I'm with some bad men, getting ready to do some bad business. I just came out to clear my mind. I've been in the joint for a while and I needed to get out and see what it's like to walk around, to be able to move about without some screw telling you where and what time to go."

"You don't look like the kind of fellow who's done time." She looked at him. "You look like a businessman. You don't talk like a hardcase either. You sound educated."

"You don't look like a street person either," he chided her. "There's no way you couldn't get cleaned up and go into some place and get a job somewhere. I know times are rough out here but you look a lot better than most. Some guy running a business would most likely hire you than some dumpy-looking dame."

"So you don't think I'm so hard on the eyes?" she said softly.

"If you look hard enough in the mirror, you could see that," he said sternly. "It's just like any other damn thing. If you're trying to sell something, you need to fix it up so someone wants to buy it. And I don't mean selling your ass, either. You fix yourself up nice, come across like a good girl, and you'll get yourself a job. Listen here, I know a couple of people over at the Villa Serena Apartments up the block. I'll go inside and see if he can let you use a couch and talk to the manager about getting a job cleaning up until you pull yourself together."

"Cleaning up?" She was disappointed. "I thought you said I was better than that."

"I didn't say that, that's what you've got in your head." Karpis scowled. "You like being out here, you call this freedom. If I got you in that hotel, you'd have enough of scrubbing and mopping and people telling you what to do in just a couple of hours. You'd be back on this street in no time, and I'd have wasted my time and money."

"Well, what about you?" she asked defensively. "You say you're going off to do a bad job somewhere. Why don't you go straight? You're halfway there already?"

There was a cop standing on the corner watching them. He probably saw her out here before and made her for a hooker. Karpis didn't need to pick up any heat out here, especially because the other guys didn't have a clue as to where he was. This flatfoot would pinch him for soliciting, and they would bring him in and find out he had no prints. He would have to get them to call Chess Power, and it would screw everything up for everyone for no good reason at all.

He wordlessly turned away from the girl, seeing the look of disappointment in her face and the cop over her shoulder about twenty yards away. He knew the bastard would swoop down on her as soon as Karpis walked off, but there was nothing he could do to change this gal's fate. She was a lost soul, searching for a place of rest that she would never allow herself to find. He never looked back, heading back to the Villa Serena, walking away from the kindred spirit that, like the cop, would forever be waiting for him right around the corner.

ↄ∕ↄↄ∕ↄ

Harry Truman had just returned from church the next morning and was watering his prize roses out in the garden of his stately home on Delaware Street near downtown Independence. His wife Bess had some business to attend to with the Women's Outreach group and was going to pick Harry up for lunch shortly.

He heard a car pull up alongside the curb and was surprised to see the four men exiting the Xenia and coming by the gate to speak with him.

"Mr. Truman?" Karpis strolled over, resplendent in his straw boater hat and bronze-colored suit. "I'm Ray Cullen and these are my associates, Clark Kent and the Plager brothers, Barclay and Bob. We've come up from San Antonio and were given your address by one of the fellows we met at your fundraiser at the Phillips last night."

"Oh, why, sure, sure, come on around." Truman was

a man of medium build, about the same size as Campbell, with the graying hair of a career politician and gold-rimmed glasses giving him the same scholastic mien as Karpis. He opened the gate and let them in, all wearing suits just like Karpis and Truman. "That's a pretty long ways up here, about a twelve-hour drive. I trust you all flew up here."

"Yeah, straight from Alcatraz." Doc grinned before Fred nonchalantly kicked the side of his shoe.

"We had some business to attend to in San Francisco and got in some sightseeing." Karpis managed a smile. "That Golden Gate Bridge sure is something. And of course, you can't leave town without taking a look at the Rock."

"Yep, great place to visit but I'm glad I'm not living there," Doc chimed in.

Truman failed to notice Fred punching him across the butt.

"Say, we heard you had a haberdashery in the down-town area," Karpis mentioned. "We've got some connections with Penner's over near the Alamo in downtown San Antonio. They've got some really great selections on tailor-made suits and I'd bet they'd go like hotcakes up here. You know how hot it is down there, having a suit's like buying an ice cream maker up in Alaska."

"I'd sure like to look into something like that." Truman smiled happily. "I closed the store back in 1922 but I've always thought of giving it another go. Say, fellow, that suitcase there looks kinda heavy. Think I can give you a hand with that?"

"Well, Senator, it's mostly brochures and the like," Campbell huffed as he lifted the bulky suitcase off the pavement. "Ray's got a couple in his jacket he can show you."

"Now, that'll be just fine," Truman replied before being distracted by the squealing of tires that disrupted the idyllic Sunday afternoon along the placid streets. "Now, what in heck? I'll bet it's those kids from Fairmount again—"

"Ray!" Fred caught a glimpse at what was careening toward the Truman home. "Hit the dirt!"

Karpis grabbed Truman in a waistlock and performed a perfect gut-wrench suplex in tossing the Missouri Senator to the ground. Campbell snapped open the suitcase so that Fred and Doc could help themselves to the Thompson submachine guns inside. Karpis rolled over and grabbed two of the guns just as the big sedan hit the brakes and its occupants charged out onto the street.

"You ever handle one of these, Senator?" Karpis asked, handing Truman one of the tommy guns.

"It's been quite a while." Truman frowned, lying on his side as he flipped the safety catch. "Of course, we didn't have anything quite this—"

Suddenly the Truman house was being riddled by automatic fire as the three gunmen sprayed the porch with bullets. The Barkers propped themselves up and returned the volley, ripping the gunman standing on the sidewalk to shreds. Karpis and Truman jumped to their feet, standing side by side as they emptied their drums into the side of the sedan before it sailed off down the road.

"Whooee!" Truman exclaimed, holding his weapon by his hip. "That sure was something! Somebody better check to see if that feller's okay. I declare, they have certainly made a mess of my home. Bess'll be fit to be tied when she comes back!"

"Well, let's get you on inside so you can give her a call first," Karpis gently relieved Truman of his weapon, making a series of hand signals to the Barkers as he steered Truman toward the house. Doc lifted the dead body by the hair into a sitting position as Fred popped the trunk open. Campbell loaded up the tommy guns and dragged the suitcase back to the Xenia, hoisting it into the trunk alongside the corpse before they slammed it shut.

"Golly gee, they have made a mess of my home!" Truman exclaimed as he viewed the devastation caused by the bullets ripping through the walls and windows.

"Think nothing of it," Karpis produced his billfold and plucked a $100 bill loose which he handed to Truman. "This should help tidy up a bit. Consider it a campaign donation."

"I'll tell you, Ray, you sure are a swell guy, and I thank you for saving my life." Truman shook his hand. "I hope to heck we see more of each other soon."

Karpis patted his shoulder. "Like I always say, when

the buck stops here, take no prisoners and get the job done."

"I'll keep that in mind." Truman smiled as they heard the wail of sirens in the distance. "Don't be a stranger, hear?"

"Did you just give that sombitch a $100 bill?" Fred asked incredulously as they took off down the road.

"Not to worry," Karpis replied. "After this is over, we'll come back down here and kidnap the sombitch and get it back."

The foursome continued on down the road on the way to their next adventure.

❧❧❧

Over a thousand miles away, a top-secret meeting was being held in Vienna, the permanent headquarters for INTERPOL. The fledgling intracontinental police organization had recently welcomed the United States as its newest member, with Assistant Director H. Drane Lester of the FBI representing America at the INTERPOL Congress in London. Despite the USA being recognized as a full-fledged participant, this discussion centered around matters posing a major threat to America's national security.

"So you have confirmed that the Russian is dead." SS General Kurt Daluege flipped through the dossier brought to his office by his visitor.

"Yes sir," SD Colonel Richard Haden replied.

Haden was recently appointed the director of SS Reichfuhrer Heinrich Himmler's Security Police and was considered a force to be reckoned with in regard to the constant power struggle within the Third Reich. His field operatives in America reported the killing of the Triad's Russian operative outside of Senator Truman's home in Independence, Missouri. "Our FBI connections reported it just hours ago. Apparently, our agent and the Italian operative escaped."

"How on earth could have they bungled such a task?" Daluege growled.

He was a man of medium build, with a receding hairline and large eyes that focused intently on those who provoked his anger. Haden had risen to such power that he was oblivious to the General's mood.

"We made it clear to them that there is a distinct possibility that Truman may be selected as the invalid Roosevelt's Vice President. Truman is a Missourian, a combative, and steadfast breed of American. If Roosevelt emerges victorious in his reelection campaign against the isolationist coward Willkie, the Americans may intervene on behalf of the British once we begin our military campaign. And if anything happens to that cripple, we will be at war with the Missourian. Colonel Haden, we cannot afford another setback. The Triad must not fail again!"

"I have every confidence in our SS operative," Haden assured Daluege, who was serving as INTER-

POL's Vice President. "Let us continue to keep our resources available in assisting the Triad as best we can, and it will be a certainty that the American war machine will fall apart before it even goes into operation."

"Good." Daluege smiled tautly. "The success of the Reich will rely on it."

℘℘℘

Doc remembered that Halloween Eve of 1938, when the Martians had attacked the planet Earth. They had directed a huge meteorite into a farm in New Jersey, and the government reported that incandescent gas explosions had been seen on the planet Mars which precipitated the attack. They were giving people instructions on how to prepare for gas attacks. Doc was in his cell in Alcatraz, and he demanded a machine gun to defend himself, but the guards refused. They had placed a radio near his cell in order to savor his terror. They probably realized they were all going to die when the Martians targeted Alcatraz. They had reconciled themselves to their fate and took delight in Doc's ill-preparedness.

The government had interrupted a live broadcast of Ramon Raquello and his Orchestra from New York's Hotel Park Plaza, so there was no way they could say it never happened. Of course, they tried to, but it was far too late. A news report told of a huge flaming object that exploded on a farm near Grovers Mill, New Jersey. A newscaster on the scene described an alien crawling out of the wreckage of a spaceship.

Doc would never forget how he told what he saw.

"God heavens, something's wriggling out of the shadow!" The man was as terrified as Doc. "It glistens like wet leather but the face—it's indescribable!"

Just last month, the government had announced a Munich Crisis overseas, telling how a man named Adolf Hitler and his army of Nazis were going to take over all of Europe. Most of the guys in Alcatraz didn't give a damn. They were on the Rock for life anyway, so maybe Hitler would let them out if he took over America. He probably would have spent so much money sending millions of men and tanks and airplanes here, he would hardly want to have to be paying for the room and board of all these convicts. Then again, if he just decided to let everyone here starve, that could be worse. For that reason, opinions in the cafeteria and on the yard were split right down the middle. Doc was astonished that everyone accepted the government's story that the whole Martian attack was a hoax. They had given away too many facts over the radio for it to be a lie. He kept it to himself and would not try to persuade anyone not to believe the government cover-up. He was truly amazed that they had pulled the wool over Ray Karpis' eyes, because Ray was the smartest guy he ever met. It was then that he suspected that they were controlling Ray's mind. Ray started talking about quantum physics, time-space continuums,

Keynesian economics, and all kinds of stuff from other planets. Neither he nor Campbell had a clue, but they yessed him to death because he was the only reality they had left to cling to.

Doc remembered going to sleep one night in January, and when he woke up he found himself in a cell on a flying saucer. They showed him a newspaper saying he had been killed in an escape attempt from Alcatraz on January thirteenth. He was frantic upon reading the headline, but they assured him he was being transported to a military base on Fort Sam Houston in San Antonio, Texas. They said the reported escape was a cover-up, just like the government saying the Martians had never really invaded. The government was going to send him, Ray, and the rest of their gang out on a secret mission to stop the Nazis from taking over the planet. He did not doubt that the Nazis were from outer space, otherwise how could they take over the planet? His suspicions were confirmed further when he found out that they had raised his brother Fred from the dead. He knew that Fred and Ma had been killed in Florida. He had seen pictures of the funeral, and even the government couldn't have faked that, any more than they could have lied about Martians or Nazis.

Ray had gotten smarter than ever, and he was talking about the government building these atomic bombs and destroying the planet. He was even dreaming about stealing one and using it to blackmail all the nations of the Earth. Fred argued that he could just as well become ruler of the world instead, but Ray said it wasn't worth the trouble. He would rather extort money from them once a year, and warn them not to make any more bombs or he would blow up the Earth. It was easy to see what made Ray so smart.

Doc also realized why Ray was insistent upon tracking down the Nazis instead of running off to take more scores instead. They would probably send flying saucers to track them down and send them to a prison on Mars. Like the government said, Martians were ugly suckers with skin like leather. If they busted out of jail, there would be no place to hide. Everyone would know they were Earthlings and not Martians. Plus, they would have no way of making a living because no one knew if there were banks on Mars. Whenever he asked someone, they acted like it was a stupid question, because how could anyone possibly know?

Doc just didn't like the fact they were back on the street and weren't able to score. He knew that Fred and Campbell probably felt the same. Doc would just bide his time until they were able to kill the Nazi Martians, known as the Triad. Once they did that, they could probably go back to knocking off banks again. Even better, if they could capture one of the flying saucers, they could go back to kidnaping. Ray always said that's where the real money was. They could transport a millionaire a week up to the ship, and in about a year they could be the richest men on Earth.

That thought made him sad. There wouldn't be any need to go running into a bank, robbing all the money, and outrunning the police after a big shootout. The world was changing much too fast. The government was taking all the fun out of life. Sometimes he just wished there were no such things as flying saucers and everything could go back to the way it was.

CHAPTER 4

Karpis and the gang pulled up in front of the Commerce Bank in Independence that Saturday morning. They had been nagging him to take a score, largely because he had to pass them chicken feed from his slowly-depleting savings funds around the country. He reluctantly agreed, and they decided on this bank on this somewhat deserted road going through town. They decided they would each carry pistols instead of tommy guns, leaving the machine guns on the seats in the Xenia covered by blankets just in case reinforcements arrived for the bank guards. It was a warm day, but the gang wore their suits and straw hats to obscure their features and hide their weapons. Karpis had come in the day before to case the place, and he assigned Fred to sit by the rear door leading to the back room where the offices, safe deposit drawers, and vault were located. He had Doc sitting on the bench facing the tellers' cages, and Campbell would stand by the front door to control traffic. Karpis would stand in the middle of the floor, all of them making busy with bankbooks and slips until Karpis made his move.

An elderly man came over by Doc and sat down alongside him on the bench in the rear. Doc was taken aback by this sudden occurrence but was experienced enough to continue fumbling with his documents.

"I remember my daddy used to bring me to this bank back when it first opened in 1905," the old man reminisced. "I was already in my forties by that time, and I never had use for banks. He tried to convince me that it was the safest place to keep your money, and that you could earn interest on your savings so that there was a little something extra come a rainy day."

"Yeah? Well, my dad never had no damn use for banks, and neither do I," Doc grunted as he decided to try and read one of the bank slips, to no avail.

"I certainly can understand why." The old man nodded sagely. "My dad decided to invest his money in stocks after he started coming here, and he was doing fine until 1929. They went and had that stock market crash, then that Depression came along. My dad was having heart trouble, and since my mom was long gone, he left all his savings in my name. He had a few thousand dollars in his name, but after that stock market crash, all he ended up leaving behind was twenty seven dollars and twenty three cents."

"That sucks," Doc said emphatically, glancing up at the old man before returning to his paperwork.

"Sure does," the man agreed. "I went ahead and left it in there to see what he was talking about. I come in here week after week to see if it grows some, and maybe about every year or so I get to take out about a quarter that come in. Otherwise, it's the same twenty seven dollars and twenty three cents."

"I'd be so pissed off if I was you, I'd get a bunch of friends together and take this place," Doc grunted, not taking his eyes off the confounding bank slips.

"You get up around my age, feller, you don't have too many friends left," he said regretfully. "I'm just too old anyway. I probably couldn't run down the street. Besides, I have no idea where I'd go. Even if I had a whole lot of money, I wouldn't have anywhere to go."

"Well, I reckon that's just about it, friend," Doc finally glanced up at him. "What would you do with all the money if you had it?"

"I don't rightly know," the man mused. "Course, if it were honestly earned, my own money, I'm sure I'd get my house fixed up nice, buy some new furniture, get a man to come on out and plant some flowers and the like. Why, I'd probably plant 'em myself just to have something to do. I might even buy myself a vehicle to drive around in, even though I'd probably grow tired of it after a while, then it'd just sit. What're you gonna do with all your money, feller?"

"What money's that?" Doc asked cautiously.

"Well, I just figured you were coming to take money out," the old man surmised. "People normally don't spend lots of time tossing money in, unless they're not careful. Don't mind my saying, but you come across as a very careful man."

Doc went back to his spurious paperwork, wondering what in hell Karpis was being so careful about.

Fred sat at the back door, going through his own notebook over and over. A young lady came over and sat down beside him. She was neatly attired in a flowered dress and straw bonnet, as if on her way to church. She daubed her forehead with a kerchief before turning to Fred, who could detect the scent of lilac in her wavy blonde hair.

She smiled pleasantly. "It's rather warm today, isn't it?"

He glanced up at her. "Sure is."

She was very cute, and if had not been such a situation as this, he would have greatly enjoyed her company. He hoped he did not have to kill her.

"I was so worried that my baby might not have handled the sun so well, I just went on and left him with my mama," she admitted. "You know how babies are, they get all cranky when they're out in the sun too long. Plus they can't tell you how they're feeling, so they just get to crying, and lots of people just feel downright uncomfortable around it. Can't say I blame them."

"Yes ma'am, that can get to be annoying," Fred agreed. "I reckon people just get to needing their space and quiet, and that kind of noise can mess things up for them."

"Oh." She caught hold of herself. "I didn't even realize. How thoughtless of me. I didn't mean to bother you."

"No, you're fine." Fred raised up resignedly, taking a break from his bogus calculations. "I was just trying to sort things out before they get to closing. The sign says they're fixing to shut 'er down about noon today."

"I'll bet you're one of those fellows who planned wisely and made his way right through that Depression without a scratch," she complimented him. "You know, even though all those people out there got all messed up, folks said that it was those who were reckless with their money in the first place, or those who never set any aside, who were the ones who got hurt the worst. Lots of people just got along like they always did, even though there wasn't a whole lot extra to go around."

"So how did your husband get you and your baby through?"

"He had a real good job with Southern Pacific Railroad, and we were holding our own until last year. There was a boiler fire that caused an explosion, and he died," she said sadly as if the memory still grieved her.

"That is a sorry situation, ma'am. I sure am sorry."

"June."

"Pardon?"

"My name's June," she said with a smile. "What's yours?"

"I'm Fred," he replied curtly, his eyes darting about to see if anyone else was within earshot.

"Are you from around here?" She wrinkled her brow. "You kinda look familiar, like I've seen you somewhere before."

"No, I've been through a number of places, but I don't reckon I've laid down stakes in Independence Springs at any time."

"You're not anyone famous, are you?" she asked shyly. "Well, that's silly. Nobody famous would come through here, much less waste time talking to me."

"I don't know why you'd say that. You're a right fine woman. Be a damn fool who wouldn't want to talk to you. Pardon my language, but I have been around hard men for a spell."

"Well, that's just fine, sir." She blushed. "Fred, I mean. I am glad to have made your acquaintance. You know, I just had a bad feeling today, and it was very unusual. Ever since I lost my husband, I resolved that I would try to see the bright side of everything, and make the best of every situation. I don't know why, but I just had this dark premonition like something bad was going to happen today, like I was going to end up in an accident somewhere. I think that's part of the reason why I left my baby home."

"I suppose I'm one of those folks who abide by such things," Fred sympathized. "My ma was like that herself. She could tell when something was about to go wrong, and I always trusted in her premonitions. You know, women do have that quality, it's what they call women's intuition. Maybe you should go on home and set with your baby for the rest of the day. That sun'll be rising up high today, and you don't need to get your pretty self all heated up."

"Why, thank you for that lovely compliment." Her eyes shone brightly. "You know, I just feel so comfortable being here talking to you, I truly feel as if the good Lord has sent you my way today. I'll just sit right here with you for a bit, and I'm sure I'll be just fine."

Fred looked over at Karpis and raised his eyebrows apprehensively, wondering what he had done to be so lucky.

Campbell was standing by the door, perusing his bankbook, just as the bank guard walked over in his ill-fitting uniform.

"Sure looks like it's gonna be a hot one out there," the guard said casually.

"Yep, sure does," Campbell replied, pretending to be distracted.

"I'll tell you, this has been my first week with this company, and this has been the best job I've had in a couple of years." The man grinned. He appeared to be a country bumpkin who may well have been hired out of desperation. "I have literally been out there breaking rocks in the heat of summer and dead of winter. Lord knows how many construction companies I've worked for, mostly mustering up at the labor office before the sun comes up every single day. I've got my missus sitting up at home with five younguns, and believe you me, it gets harder and harder to bring home enough to go around. Job like this makes you feel a whole lot better knowing there's a set amount you'll be able to count on."

"Well, I can certainly understand that," Campbell replied testily. "I just wonder why a man with five kids would place himself at risk taking a job like this. Suppose a desperate man came walking in here expecting to come away with a score, having as great a need as someone like yourself? It's not always a John Dillinger or a Harry Campbell who is just looking for some extra seed money to spend at the whorehouse. Suppose a man who had no other way to go came through here? Would whatever the Pinkertons pay you be worth it?"

"Well, heck, mister, that would be a very unfortunate thing to happen," the man said quietly, shaking his head. "I guess it'd kinda be like having a load fall on you on the jobsite, or slipping and falling while you're carrying something. It'd be kinda like an act of God, I suppose there'd be nothing you could do about it. You know, like a man walking across a field in the rain every month of his life, and the one time he just gets struck by lightning. You can sit back and say you should've done this or that, but after all is said and done, it's just your day that's come."

"Well, suppose you knew that load was about to fall, or you knew that pothole was sitting there awaiting, or you knew those bank robbers were coming through?" Campbell insisted. "Would you be dumb enough to go right on with what you were doing, or would you be thinking about your family and avoid the pitfall?"

"That is a helluva question, sir." The guard rubbed his chin. "A helluva question."

Campbell looked over beseechingly at Karpis, wondering just if and when they would be helping this poor soul find the answer that evaded him.

Karpis met Campbell's gaze and closed his eyes for a long moment. He felt a cold chill go down his spine and reopened them at once, finding himself in a dark room. He rolled to his feet and lurched across the floor, out into the moonlit hallway before him.

"Can't sleep again?" Fred asked, sitting by a window, smoking a cigarette.

"I was doing okay. Had a weird dream."

"Thinking about taking a score?"

"Not right now, not just yet," Karpis admitted, staring out along with Fred at the geese swimming along the moonlit creek outside their townhouse at the Country Club Plaza.

"Think we'll ever get around to it again?" Fred asked.

"Hell, who knows? Things are so screwed up these days, it's not just about walking into a bank, or what you might be facing when you come out. We could have a bigger problem dealing with who got there before us."

"Well, I guess I'd like to see about that," Fred scoffed.

"Maybe you won't." Karpis chuckled back. "Maybe you don't."

೮ᕲ೮ᕲ

Feta had pulled up to the Truman house in his taxi-cab, paying the driver before it did a U-turn and cruised away from the commotion. It was right after hearing of the incident on the radio that same afternoon. The place was fairly well cordoned off by the police, and neighbors flocked around to ensure their beloved Trumans were okay. Feta took a circular route by the corner, but at once felt the presence of a man behind him sticking a gun barrel into his ribs.

"Okay, buddy," the assailant muttered. "Head to that black car by the curb and get in nice and easy. You make a move or start yelling and I'll blow your guts out."

Feta knew that this was the fatal hazard of his profession. This could easily be someone who held a grudge from a previous job, or any one of a number of fugitives who might have considered this a preemptive strike. He knew that if it had to do with the Karpis ringer, all he had to do was let them know he was backed by the Genoveses and that should get him off the hook. The best he could do was hope and pray that his luck was still holding out.

The gunman ushered him to the Cadillac and opened the door for him. He got in the back seat next to a second man who had his hand in his black suit jacket. The first man slipped into the passenger seat before the car cruised off.

"Where we headed?" Feta managed as the car circled the block and headed back toward KC.

"That's the least of your worries." The man seated next to him showed the butt of a gun inside his jacket.

They continued the ride in silence and drove back toward town before veering off onto Broadway. From there they turned off along Twelfth Street and headed down toward the notorious West Bottoms area of downtown.

"I hope you guys are getting a good deal on the rent down here," Feta grunted as the car pulled up into what seemed to be a deserted warehouse.

The gunman got out and unlocked the front door, then came back for Feta as they hustled him in under tight guard.

The lead man switched on a dim light, and they brought him in to a darkened room where a man in a dark suit sat in the shadows behind a desk. The gunman prodded him over to the chair before the desk as the rest of them took positions around the room.

"Bob Feta," the average-built man said crisply. "Cat the Bounty Hunter. Your reputation precedes you. I'm wondering how you got to where you're tracking down guys who don't have prices on their heads. Wishful thinking, perhaps?"

"So let me guess. Are you from the License Bureau?"

"We'll cross that bridge shortly. Don't tell me you're doing this out of boredom. Let me ask who you think's gonna pay you for whatever info you're looking for?"

"I've already got a buyer," Feta said curtly. "There's some bad people paying for this info. Why're you dealing yourself into this game for?"

"We'll ask the questions, scumbag," the gunman growled.

The man at the desk rested his chin on his palm. "You can either tell us who's paying, or my friend can rip it outta you."

"Joe Adonis outta New York," Feta said cautiously.

"Adonis," the man grunted. "That brings the whole slimebucket into the mix: Buchalter, Anastasia, Lansky, and Siegel. Hard to believe the whole pack of rats're turning on Charlie Lucky."

Feta held his palm up. "Hey, all I do is pass along info. What they do with it's not my business."

"We're planning to make it ours," the man retorted.

"I'm Jack Mulligan with the Irish Mob in New York. We've been standing on the sidelines for years now, and it finally looks like the greaseballs are starting to backstab each other for a change. We didn't mind Charlie Lucky. He was a pretty fair guy, all in all. That piece of crap Genovese, though, that's a different story. If Charlie loses in court, that's one thing. We don't want to see him take a bum rap, though, and that looks like what the Sicilian Mob is setting him up for."

"Sicilian Mob?" Feta squinted. "That's Luciano's power base, that's who he's going back to if he gets set up. You don't mean—"

"Exactly." Mulligan nodded. "We think Genovese reached past Luciano and made a connection in Sicily. They've got a hit squad here in the States making moves, and they're going on a killing spree that Charlie's gonna get framed for. That Karpis copycat crew you're after is most likely the cleanup team. They knock off any survivors or witnesses, and if they don't do their job, they take the rap for what the heavy hitters did."

"So why would..." Feta's voice trailed off as a glint of realization came to his eyes.

"Now you see it, don'tcha?" Mulligan smiled. "Genovese has you tailing the Karpis ringers to make sure they don't leave any traces behind."

"But I went to Genovese, not the other way around."

"He's a slippery snake, that one. He would've come to you in time. This is why you need us standing behind you, to make sure he doesn't dispose of you when he's done with you."

"This is clear as mud." Feta grew exasperated. "So who the hell is the hit squad?"

"It's an espionage team known as the Triad." The gunman walked over to the table. He was a tall, gray-haired man with big, icy-blue eyes. "They've been suspected of dozens of political murders throughout Europe since the fascist regimes began coming to power over this decade. There's a Russian, a German, and an Italian assassin on the team, and these guys are bad news. The Russian is Vladimir Markoff, an NKVD—that's the People's Commissariat of Internal Affairs—agent. The German is Eric Von Hoffman, a Waffen-SS commando, and we believe the Italian is Emiliano Murra, a Sardinian hit man from the Camorra or Sicilian Mafia. These guys are three of the worst killers on the face of the planet. The penalty for failure is death where these guys come from, and obviously they've never failed in nearly ten years. We don't know who they're here to kill or what they're planning, but those Karpis impostors are hot on their tail, and we want to tie you onto theirs."

"This sounds like nasty stuff," Feta mused. "What's in it for me?"

"Your life," Mulligan snapped. "Once you run down the Karpis ringers and pin the tail on the donkey, or the Triad in this case, you can hide behind us and the Genoveses won't try to cover their tracks with you on top of them. Plus, I'll see to it that we've got a little something for you if Genovese doesn't pay whatever he promised."

"Okay." Feta exhaled tautly. "I don't suppose I have any choice here. I know if I went back to the Genoveses with this, I wouldn't walk out alive, if what you're telling me is on the level."

"You can take a chance, which I know you won't," Mulligan said smugly, "or you can come in with me, which I'm pretty sure you will. Of course, you can leave town, but I think you're pretty comfortable here in KC and don't want to leave home, am I right?"

Feta cleared his throat. "Yeah, yeah."

"Good," Mulligan beamed. "You're hired."

പ്രേ

Karpis and his men drove up to Kearney, the birthplace of Jesse James, whose criminal elements still took pride in that claim to fame. Karpis knew of an abortion doctor in the area, a failed practitioner who had taken to drink but had been known as one of the best in the business. Among his many talents was experience in forensics. He took the corpse from the trunk of the Xenia and did an autopsy in his garage as Karpis and the others waited in a tavern up the street.

"Okay, Ray." The curly-haired, bespectacled doctor met with Karpis in his back yard after the task was completed. "Here's your autopsy report, fingerprints, and my observations. Just give me my fee and your guarantee this one doesn't turn up anywhere within a hundred miles of here. Well, then again, let's make it two hundred, for obvious reasons."

"Yeah, the coppers probably won't buy into the idea that some kid outta med school got hold of this stiff and used it for practice," Karpis smirked, handing him $500. "You're a prince, Doc. If I get any goodies, theatre tickets or anything down this way, I'll mail 'em over."

The doc chuckled. "I'm not sure I'm gonna be looking forward to getting mail from Alvin Karpis."

"Karpis!" Karpis looked around furtively. "You mean he broke outta Alcatraz?"

The men shook hands and patted each other's shoulders before Karpis took his leave.

"So where we dumping this stiff?" Doc asked as he and Fred put the blanket-wrapped corpse back in the trunk of the Xenia.

"Fred, why don't you call those guys you lined up over on Troost Avenue?" Karpis suggested. "This'll be their initiation. The torso's pretty well scooped out, so just have them take off the head, the arms and legs, and make them disappear in opposite directions. I'd give 'em about fifty bucks apiece. Tell 'em they'll be active members of the Barker Gang."

"Oh, so now it's the *Barker* Gang," Fred raised his eyebrows. "What happened to the *Karpis*-Barker Gang that was terrorizing the Midwest?"

"Karpis?" Karpis squinted? "That poor mook's doing life on the Rock. Just ask Doc."

"You mean they caught *another* one?" Doc was incredulous.

Fred made a few calls and soon they were on their way down US Highway 40 back to the downtown KC area. They cruised down Troost Avenue to the tavern where Fred had gone recruiting and came across the five hardcases he had prospected.

They were eager to get involved and gladly took the disposal job for $50 per man.

Just as Fred had anticipated, they took just as much pleasure in carving up the corpse as they did making the money for the job. Fred told him they would be in touch, and they were greatly looking forward to hearing from him soon.

Karpis next contacted a bookmaking operation who had a teleprinter on site and paid them to transmit the information from the doctor's autopsy findings to his Dragnet connection. They next returned to the Plaza for a late dinner and ruminated over the day's events.

Campbell shook his head as he dug into his plate of linguini and meat sauce at the Italian Gardens on Baltimore Avenue. "I'll tell you, Ray, there's never a dull moment with you around. Having a gunfight at Senator Truman's house, driving a stiff around in the trunk all afternoon, then driving it down to Gangland to have it chopped up. Typical Sunday, huh?"

"What'd you rather be doing, reading your Bible on the Rock and waiting for lockdown?" Karpis growled, sipping his coffee. "Like you said, it's Sunday, so count your blessings."

"Geez, Ray, I got blood all over my new suit jacket," Doc griped, causing Karpis's eyes to dart about frantically for signs of eavesdroppers.

"For crying out loud, Freddie, did this guy come with a leash and muzzle?" Karpis hissed at him.

"C'mon, Ray, relax. You worry too much." Fred lit up a cigarette after sipping a glass of vintage Merlot. "You'd better eat some of that godam food. You're gonna waste away to nothing."

"Yeah, right." Karpis picked at his plate of scungilli, though as usual he would probably only eat a couple of bites. "I'm gonna have to call my connection and see what they came up with on that report, then touch bases with Power and see if they've got anything new on that end."

"You know what your problem is, Ray?" Campbell munched on a piece of sausage. "It's all business with you. If Betty Grable came over here and laid one of her gams up on the table in front of you, you'd probably get out a pen and start mapping out a bank job on it."

"Yeah? Well, I heard Twentieth Century Fox took out a million-dollar insurance policy on those legs," Karpis replied. "I think I'd get together with her and figure out how we could swindle 'em for the score. After that, I'd have plenty of money and time to mix a whole lotta pleasure with business."

"You got a way with words, you old hound dog," Fred chortled.

Karpis did his best to take his mind off business as they laughed and traded jokes, finishing their meal before heading back to the Plaza. Karpis's townhouse was a luxurious place replete with a high-ceilinged living room with chandelier and fireplace surrounded by stone-paved flooring. He lit the fireplace with a tiny fire for ambiance as the others lounged around the balcony enjoying the magnificent view of the Plaza storefronts overlooking the moonlit creek. Karpis dutifully got on the phone and, after a series of calls, came up with the info he wanted.

The dead man was indeed one Captain Vladimir Markoff, who had come to the US with a diplomatic visa right after the Russian Revolution in 1929 where he served as a lowly lieutenant. Apparently, he joined the NKVD and worked his way up the ranks through espionage and murder. This would validate Power's theory about some mysterious Triad having snuck into the country to bump off some unknown targets. Obviously Truman was one of them, and Markoff paid the price for that screwup.

Karpis's connections were now looking out for a dark Cadillac along the Highway 40 corridor with bullet holes needing repair. He doubted very much that these fellows would have done a U-turn and tried to negotiate a

roadblock between Kansas and Missouri, with cops probably crawling all over trying to find out who tried to
waste Truman. Plus, there weren't any decent targets out
there. They had to be going back East, and if they had
any decent safe houses, at least one would be located in
St. Louis. That, Karpis decided, was exactly where he
and the boys needed to go.

୧୨୧୨

They pulled over about halfway to St. Louis at a gas
station along the outskirts of the little college town of Co-
lumbia.

Fred went inside and paid for gas and beer while
Campbell and Doc headed to some nearby bushes to re-
lieve themselves. Karpis's core values did not allow for
him to piss in public, so he withstood the stench of the
outhouse before wandering around the side of the building where a disheveled young fellow was sitting.

"So what's your story?" Karpis asked casually.

"Well, the factory I'd been working at since I got out
of high school closed down about a month ago," the man
replied as he sat on the ground, leaning against the wall.
"My dad worked there, and my granddaddy before him.
Damned sombitchin' government kept on taxing the
place into the ground, never once letting up even with the
company losing money the way they were. Even the ex-
ecutives were giving up all kinds of raises and perks the

last couple of years from what we heard, trying to keep the place open. They finally closed the doors, and when I lost my job, my wife took the kids and ran out on me. She said she'd rather live off handouts from her folks than watch her kids run around in rags with nothing to eat."

"That's cold shit, fellow." Karpis shook his head. "I suppose it's a lot harder to start a new family than to find a new girl. The way things are these days, even that may be harder than finding a new job. You gotta keep your head up, though. The minute you go down, there's nobody that'll help you get back up. Everybody's fighting too hard to stay on their own two feet these days."

The man looked up at him. "Say, you're Alvin Karpis, aren't you?"

"Yeah, well, keep it to yourself," Karpis replied then, as an afterthought, pulled his .38 Smith and Wesson out of his waistband and held it grip first toward the man. "You know, you don't have to accept things the way they are. Desperate times call for desperate measures."

"You certainly are right," the man agreed, taking the revolver from Karpis and checking to see if it was loaded. "Say, now, I'd bet I could make a pretty penny just by turning you in for the reward."

"Yeah, you might." Karpis stood with his fists on hips, looking down at the man. "Problem is, if I'm Karpis, then I probably got the Barkers and Harry Campbell with me, or any one of the other thirty guys in our gang. Just something to think about."

"That's true," the man said, the gun barrel pointed at the ground in front of Karpis.

"Plus, in my way of thinking, a guy who wouldn't have stopped a gal from walking out on him with his own kids wouldn't put a bullet in someone," Karpis pointed out. "That's not necessarily a judgment of character, but it's a deciding factor for someone who might be putting themselves in front of a bullet. I don't think you're ready to point a gun at someone at this point in your life."

"You're right, Mr. Karpis," the man turned the gun around and handed the grip back to Karpis. "I ain't no killer."

"Neither am I, fellow," Karpis replied. "I'm lucky I've never found a man who's given me a reason to make me one. Tell you what, when you've grown the balls to kill a man, go after that wife and kids of yours first. It takes more guts to keep a family together in this economy than to pull a trigger on a gun."

"I will keep that in mind, Mr. Karpis." The man looked up at him, offering his hand in friendship.

Karpis took his hand and pulled him to his feet. "Don't look up to no one," he told him. "You stand square with them and look them in the eye. Your kids need you to be strong for them so they can be strong for you. You get yourself together and get them back so they can hold you up."

"Thanks, Mr. Karpis," the man said earnestly.

Karpis patted his shoulder before rejoining his partners and driving off into the night.

ↄ৲ↄ৲ↄ

Right about that time, Adonis was on the phone at his luxury suite at the Savoy Hotel, giving a detailed report to one of his most feared associates in NYC. Albert Anastasia was the Boss of one of the Five Families, known as the Mad Hatter for his predilection for having people killed for reasons known only to himself. Most people tried to deal with his Underboss, Carlo Gambino, whenever possible, but in this case Anastasia insisted on personally handling the matter.

"I'm tellin' you, Albert, this guy Cat the Bounty Hunter has an excellent rep out here. It's like he always gets his man, like on those radio shows. He was just behind that shootout at the Truman house, he got there right after the cops showed up. If that stickup gang is out working on a hit list, this guy is gonna help us figure out who's on it."

"And I'm tellin' *you*, Joey, my ace is with Charlie." Anastasia snarled. "I'm not standin' by if anybody's got any ideas of whackin' him out or framin' him for a political assassination! You make sure Vito understands that, and tell him that goin' behind my back to talk to Carlo ain't gonna get it either! If anything happens to Charlie before or after his trial, there's gonna be a pile of bodies out in the friggin' street!"

"Take it easy, Albert," Adonis pleaded. "Why do you think we got this guy on that gang's tail feathers? We wanna know where they're going and make sure nobody's trying to mess with Charlie, just like you!"

"That's how it better play out, Joey," Anastasia growled. "We voted Charlie in as the head of the Syndicate, and that was unanimous. You try to take a Boss out, this whole thing of ours ain't worth crap. If anybody—and I mean *anybody*—moves on Charlie, then they move on me."

"Relax, Al," Adonis said, trying to placate him before hanging up. "As soon as we get anything else you'll be the first to know."

Genovese and Buchalter were sitting with Adonis in his suite. Genovese shook his head as Adonis hung up. "Mad Hatter is right. Between him and Bugsy Siegel, I don't know who's nuttier. You know, it's like we were talkin' about before. Suppose Mussolini and those screwballs in the Old Country are behind this? We already know they're cracking down on the Camorra in Sicily. Those fascist bastards have half the old-time Godfathers in jail. Lookit that, you got Anastasia, you got Siegel, you got Mussolini, if they got their way, half the world would be six feet under."

"You're right," Adonis replied. "If the fascists put out a hit on Charlie for whatever reason and get the job done, it's gonna start a war with the Anastasias. We gotta make sure that Feta guy gets full support out there. We gotta make sure he stays glued to that machine-gun gang. Who knows, maybe we might think about taking them out ourselves."

"That's a Mad Hatter move, Joey," Buchalter said, his boyish features twisted into a scowl. "Even Charlie and Meyer Lansky would be against that. The last thing we need is Hoover having second thoughts about us even existing. You know that if this thing is leading to a political assassination, we need to keep as far from it as possible."

"Okay," Genovese relented. "Just keep tabs on this Cat of yours. We gotta stay all over this thing and find out where it's going. And, by the way, get in touch with Al Capone's contacts in Alcatraz."

"Capone?" Adonis wondered.

"I want to make sure that son of a bitch Karpis is still there," Genovese fumed, knowing that it was always best to be safe than sorry, especially when Mob bosses and state senators were showing up on the firing lines.

ℰↈℰↈ

Karpis and his men decided to spend the night in St. Charles, a small town located northwest of St. Louis along the Missouri River. There was a hotel conveniently located in the downtown area, and Karpis checked them in before stepping outside for a cigarette. There was a saloon a couple of doors from the hotel, and the boys decided to stop in for a drink before calling it a night.

He stood out on the boardwalk outside Boone's Colonial Inn where he spotted a forlorn young woman dressed in threadbare clothes, sitting by a row of bushes as if her world had fallen apart. She gazed despairingly out at the river, as if all hope was lost, and barely noticed Karpis until she saw his highly-buffed shoes standing alongside her.

"Good evening, sir," she said with a hint of an Irish accent, her blue eyes shining bright as her titian tresses cascaded around her pretty face. "Certainly is a lovely evening."

"Sure is," he grunted. "What're you sitting out here alone for, all down in the dumps?"

"I just arrived here from St. Louis, hoping my luck might change," she sighed. "This Depression just seems to grind folks into the dust, and set people in the worst moods against one another. I was unable to find any gainful employment, and the charity houses are overwhelmed by the needy. I decided to come up here out of desperation, and it seems I can't find a place for myself here either."

"Do you know who I am?" he asked her, stepping down into the lamplight so she could get a good look at him.

"No sir, but you do seem familiar," she rose from where she was sitting to her five-foot-six-inch height. She had a fine figure and alabaster skin that had been somewhat tarnished by the sun.

"I'm Alvin Karpis," he growled. "And you must be stupid."

"Why, yes, Alvin Karpis, I have heard of you," she managed, taken aback. "Now, sir, why must be insulting toward me? I've done you no harm."

"You do yourself harm by sitting around feeling sorry for yourself," he snapped at her. "Have you ever seen a cat or a dog, or a bird in a tree having a pity party? There's bums lined up at every soup kitchen across the country crying over spilled milk. A beautiful girl like you shouldn't lower yourself to that level."

"Well, sir," she said defensively, "looks aren't everything."

"They're at least half the battle as far as dames are concerned," he retorted. "Plus, you just got through saying you weren't stupid. So why aren't you getting ahead?"

She lowered her eyes. "People just need a little bit of a break to get by these days. It just takes that tiny bit of luck to get spotted by the foreman though you've mustered at the job site hours before the work call. It's often by chance that one manages to arrive at the boarding house right after they've run out of room. I'm not one to say that all the grapes are sour, but surely a lass can't be put to scorn if she is discouraged over being short-changed time and again."

"Bah, that's a lot of hooey." Karpis scowled, digging into his pocket for his billfold. "See here. I'll give you a couple of bucks and an address and phone number to check out. You take the train back to St. Louis and call this number when you get there, let them know you're in town before you show up. You go and get yourself some nice clothes, buy a pretty dress and get yourself a room. My friends will make sure you meet the right people and get hooked up with a good job. After that, you're on your own, understand?"

He pulled a $50 from his wallet and handed it to her. She stared at it aghast before dropping to her knees and wrapping her arms around his legs.

"Oh, Mr. Karpis," she wept, holding her face against his thighs. "You are truly a saint. How can I ever thank you? How could I repay you?"

"I thought you said you weren't stupid." He gently pushed her shoulders away, wrote an address and phone number down on a piece of paper he pulled from his pocket, and handed it to her. "Go on and catch that last train before you get stuck here another night. If you ever read in the papers where I got caught somewhere, just be sure and send a nice letter to the governor in that state."

"Thank you and God bless you, Mr. Karpis." Tears of joy rolled down her cheeks. "I'll never forget you."

"Yeah, just be careful. Tell 'em Ray sent you." He

waved goodbye before he went back inside the hotel. As soon as she disappeared down the street, Karpis asked the desk clerk for a telephone and was directed to a booth in a far corner.

"Connery's Pub," said the man who answered the St. Louis phone number he dialed.

"This is Karpis."

"Ray! Are you kidding? When the hell did you get out?"

"Keep it to yourself, nobody knows, not even the cops," he ordered. "Look, I got this girl coming into town on the train either tonight or tomorrow. She's a nice look-ing redhead, a distant relative of mine. I want you guys to put her up and help her get situated. I won't mind if she meets up with a nice fellow, either."

The man chuckled. "I'm sure that can be arranged."

"Listen here, no funny stuff," Karpis warned him. "They'd better treat her like royalty. If I find out other-wise, I'll send some of the guys over there. Not only will they open some skulls, but you'll be standing in a crater. Understand?"

"Hey, c'mon, Ray," the man pleaded. "How long have you known me? I'll treat her like my kid sister. You can bet on it."

"I'm holding you to it," Karpis assured him before hanging up.

Doc came into the lobby followed by Fred and Campbell. "C'mon, Ray," Doc said. "We're waiting on you. What're you doing, placing a bet? Somebody give you a hot tip on a race horse?"

"Yeah, a pretty little filly," Karpis replied as he headed out the door alongside them. "She's a sure winner. I'd bet fifty bucks on her."

"Well, why don't you let us in on it?" Harry insisted.

"What can I say?" Karpis asked with a shrug. "I didn't even get her name."

ღღღ

The townhouse at the Plaza had taken on a psychedelic quality for Karpis. At night, after the others had gone to bed, the spacious living room had an ultraviolet fluorescence as the moonlight played with the shadows. It was almost like staring at a fish tank long enough to make one think they had dozed off, then woke up inside it. When he dreamed of Alcatraz and woke up in a cold sweat, trying to remember if he was here or back there, he would wander into the living room. Sometimes it made him feel as if he was still dreaming. He woke up and found himself in broad daylight, staring out the windshield of an automobile.

Only the air conditioner was much more powerful than he was used to and the smell of the car was different. He looked out the passenger window and somehow things seemed different.

They were in a black neighborhood, but the cars

seemed a lot newer than they should have been. They were better-looking than the car the gang was sitting in.

"I was just gonna wake you up," Doc said as he lit a cigarette.

"Who the hell let you drive?" Karpis blinked, rubbing his eyes, turning around to see Freddie and Campbell in the back seat.

They were looking out their windows, immersed in thought as they usually were before jobs.

"You did. You said you needed Harry at the door and Freddie inside with you."

Karpis broke out in a cold sweat, and this time he wasn't dreaming—or was he? No matter how strung out things had gotten, he would have never planned a job with just four guys. It took at least six guys to take a score, all the yeggs knew that. He was trying to remember where they were and what job this was, but he wasn't about to appear weak before the others. He knew it would come to him eventually. He would just have to let his head clear.

"Okay." Doc pulled over and parked about twenty yards from a brick and mortar building that had the words Freedom National Bank on the sign over the entrance situated between two massive pillars. This was undoubtedly a black neighborhood, and he had never seen such a display of prosperity in such an area in his life. "Let's go to work."

"Hold on," Karpis protested as the guys got out of

the car. "You telling me you couldn't get any of those fellows from Troost to come and help out?"

"Not all the way up to Harlem." Fred pulled two satchels along with two odd-looking rifles and two over-coats out of the trunk. "You were the one who said it wouldn't work anyway."

"Harlem?" Karpis got out, staring at the odd cut of their suits, the strange advertising in the store windows, the weird devices the black kids were messing with as they walked up and down the street. Something was wrong here, but there were no cops anywhere. He couldn't call this off as much as his instincts were screaming that he do so. He walked around and was handed one of the rifles. It was surprisingly lightweight with a fair-sized clip, and he was wondering where the hell they got them from. Doc got back into the car with his rifle, and Karpis started toward the bank when at once the alarms started going off. The gang watched in aston-ishment as a convoy of police cars and trucks appeared out of nowhere, cordoning off both ends of the street as cops began pouring onto the street with guns drawn.

"What the hell's up, Ray?" Fred exclaimed. "They got us surrounded!"

Suddenly four black guys with odd-looking machine guys stormed out of the bank carrying their scores in can-vas bags. They were wearing T-shirts, jeans, and sneak-ers, and began spraying automatic fire on the police vehi-cles as the cops ducked for cover. Karpis looked around

and saw the officers zeroing in on them, thinking they
had something to do with it.

"You men beside the Lexus!" a bullhorn blared. "Put
down whatever you're carrying and put your hands in the
air!"

Doc looked around. "What Lexus?"

"Kiss my ass!" Fred yelled, opening up a volley of
rifle fire on the police. Karpis was impressed by the fluid-
ity of the rifle, the accuracy, and the damage it inflicted.
It was a whole lot better than those Browning Automatic
Rifles those kids from Texas, Bonnie and Clyde, tried to
foist on him last year.

"Hey, dogs!" one of the black kids called out as they
ran down the street toward them, only racing up the steps
to a nearby brownstone building. "C'mon in here and we
can hold them off long enough to break out the back!"

Karpis stared at the buildings on the block—most of
them painted with obscure lettering and symbols, the like
of which he had never seen before. Some of the buildings
had been boarded up with wood and sheet metal, like this
one the kids were breaking into. Karpis saw no choice but
to follow the kids up the steps of the brownstone, through
the front door.

"What the hell you guys doing up here?" the leader
of the black gangsters asked as they raced down the peel-
ing, urine-soaked corridor.

"That's a damned good question," Karpis replied.
"Somebody gave me one crappy tip."

"Glad to hear you didn't just dream it up," Freddie grunted.

One of the black kids kicked down a door at the end of the hall, and a mother and her kids inside began squealing as the gangsters rushed in. Karpis and the boys rushed in behind them as the leader smashed out a window so that they could climb out onto the fire escape.

"Geez, ever hear of opening the window?" Campbell grumbled as Karpis and the others followed them out.

They could see the police rushing out the back exits of the bank, and the black kids began pouring fire down on them so that they ran for cover. These situations always reminded Karpis of a peashooter fight: first there was one ping, then another and, suddenly, it was like a hailstorm around where they stood. The blacks scampered up the fire escape, and Karpis and the boys followed until they were standing on the roof. They joined the gangsters in shooting down at the police, until at once, a flying vehicle resembling a mechanical locust began swooping down on them.

"What the hell is that?" the boys cried out.

"What it look like, you stupid hillbillies? It's a police helicopter! C'mon, we gotta jump across to the other roof!" the leader yelled.

The kids began jumping, one by one, onto the next door roof that was about twenty feet below from the south parapet.

"We're done, Ray!" Campbell gasped as he considered the jump. "Maybe those monkeys made it, but that fall will break our legs!"

"I'd rather go inside with a broken leg than get taken in wondering whether I could've made it," Karpis snapped.

At once he stepped up onto the parapet and jumped off, landing on the rooftop below with a brutal impact. His legs buckled when he hit, and his body bounced off the tarpaper as he lost his grip on his rifle. The wind was knocked out of him and he fought to keep from slipping into unconsciousness...

"Hey, Ray," he heard Fred calling him gently. "You awake?"

"What—" Karpis looked around, finding himself back in the dream house on the Plaza. "Yeah, yeah, I'm good."

"Having another bad dream?"

"I guess so," Karpis looked around. "I must be sleepwalking or something. I didn't even know I came down here."

"Yeah, it happens to me too," Fred seemed to always be looking out that same patio window, smoking the same cigarette, staring at the same thing.

Only this time Karpis could not see Fred's reflection, and as he rubbed his eyes it was still not visible. "Say, Fred, can you get me my smokes over there on the table by the fireplace?"

Fred walked over and frowned as the pack was not

there. Karpis blanched as he stared at the mirror over the fireplace and still saw no reflection. "Fred," Karpis managed. "Where's your reflection? In the mirror?"

"Right there." Fred looked up and smoothed his hair. "You got no smokes over here. Take one of mine."

He brought the pack over and stared at Karpis quizzically as he grabbed Fred's wrist while pulling a Chesterfield out of his pack.

"Just making sure I'm not out Nazi hunting with a damned ghost," Karpis smirked.

"You're starving yourself to death, and you're losing your mind," Fred lit Karpis's cigarette. "What're you wearing, size 27 pants? I know broads who're bigger than you."

"I've seen the broads you go out with, those heifers are all bigger than you." Karpis chuckled weakly. He could still not reconcile himself to Fred having no reflection.

"I've been having the same dreams you have." Fred resumed his spot by the window again. "I dreamed we were doing a job in uptown Manhattan, knocking off a bank in some black neighborhood. They got ambushed by the coppers and we were smack dab in the middle of it."

"Wait a second. I didn't tell you what I was dreaming."

"I know it." Fred exhaled a stream of smoke, and it occurred to Karpis that a ghost couldn't smoke a cigarette. "Maybe it's some kind of government mind control thing, like they have on those radio shows. Maybe the army guys let the Hoover boys get inside Fort Sam and mess around with my brain. They may be transmitting some kind of brain waves that are getting intercepted by that computer brain of yours."

"How do you know about computers?"

"Whaddaya think, I'm stupid? I listen to *Flash Gordon* on the radio and read *Buck Rogers* in the funny papers. I know more about culture than you think."

"All right, simmer down. So go on and figure, how would Hoover know about them flying machines, those helicopters?"

"Maybe the army has them as some kind of secret weapon, like those atom bombs they keep talking about in them science fiction books."

"No way. If they had them they would've used them on us long ago. Let me tell you, when Hoover nailed me, he was pissed. If he would've had a helicopter, I wouldn't have seen one fed coming across the street at me. They would've wiped me off the map first."

"They might be reading my mind right now, listening in on us," Fred mused.

"How can he be mindreading a ghost?" Karpis scoffed. "I'm going to bed. I'm the only one in this room who's going crazy."

Fred waved him off. "If I'm a ghost, you *are* the only one in the room."

Karpis made his way back to his bedroom and wondered whether or not all this had to do with Einstein's theory on the time-space continuum and the fourth dimension. He would double-check his science journal tomorrow, even though it wouldn't make a damn bit of difference. They still had a job to do.

CHAPTER 5

The Mayfair Hotel had become one of St. Louis's most prestigious hotels over its fourteen-year history. Built in the Italian Renaissance architecture style with mat-faced brick and terra cotta trim, its copper canopies gave it a majestic ambiance visible from blocks away throughout the downtown area. It was one of Karpis's favorite stopovers while traveling, and he headed straight there, though he allowed Campbell to approach the desk to make the arrangements. Karpis was getting too many remarks about resembling Alvin Karpis and decided to keep a lower profile.

After renting the three rooms—one to be shared by the Barkers so Fred could watch over Doc—they took the short drive down to Laclede's Landing, the cobblestoned area near the Mississippi docks where Hannegan's Restaurant was located. There was a large Irish community in the area and the food was old country authentic, reminding him of some of his Mom's recipes when he was a boy in Topeka. As they always said, he ate like a bird, but when he came to Hannegan's he always took more than a few bites.

"So did you get anything new on those Triad guys?" Fred asked as he munched on his sirloin steak. "That shootout at Truman's must have made some kind of changes in their game plans. They can't be thinking four guys with Tommy guns sittin' at Truman's waiting for 'em was some kind of accident."

"It's not so much about what they might be thinking as what we make them think." Karpis savored his shepherd pie. The high-ceilinged, wood-paneled, mirror-decorated restaurant was just as comfortable as any in the Midwest and the wait staff was courteous and attentive. The well-dressed foursome was as inconspicuous as any other, and they were relaxed in determining their next course of action. "First thing they'll do is report to their bosses and see if they've got a leak somewhere. No way they're gonna think it was a coincidence. Next thing they'll do is try and move ahead of schedule to get the jump on us. Beyond that, if I was their boss, I'd be making plans to figure out how to help them shake their tail. In which case, we'd better keep our eyes open and stay on our toes."

"Well, they know we're armed to the teeth, so if they come at us, they'll be hauling some heavy metal in with 'em," Campbell decided. "You know, if we're really playing some kind of spy game, I'm not sure they're gonna want to get into a machine gun fight with us. Those cloak-and-dagger guys like to do things on the sneak, like poison or strangle each other. If you listen to any of those spy shows on the radio, that's mostly what they're good at."

"C'mon, Harry." Karpis waved him off. "Suppose they decided to send Indian assassins after us. You think they'd be shooting arrows or trying to scalp us? Those radio shows are a lot of hooey."

"I'm not lettin' no godam Injuns peel off my scalp, that's for damn sure," Doc growled.

"You see?" Karpis looked at Campbell, pointing at Doc. "See what you started?"

The waitress brought a second round of drinks as the gang finished their meals. Unknown to them, the members of the Triad who had escaped the gun battle at Truman House reported the presence of a man who looked just like Alvin Karpis. The Nazi spy network put out the word, and sympathizers throughout Missouri were looking out for anyone who fit that description. As a result, a man who happened to be on Laclede's Landing that evening happened to spot someone looking like Karpis. He called his own connection and, within a short while, a Nazi collaborator came out to investigate.

"Excuse me, sir." A tall gentleman with a thick German accent came up to their table. "Are you Alvin Karpis?"

"Nah, I'm Dillinger." Karpis put on his glasses. "Karpis is staying over at the Frisco Hotel in Valley Park. We were trying to tell the dumbass there were no banks to knock over in those parts."

"I just couldn't resist." The man chuckled. "You really must hear that a lot. You look just like him. I didn't mean to interrupt your dinner. Have a wonderful evening."

"Okay guys, sit tight." Karpis waited until the man left the restaurant. "I'm gonna tail that son of a bitch."

"Why don't you let me watch your back," Fred insisted.

"Two guys on his ass would be too obvious," Karpis said, picking a steak knife off the table. "If I'm not back in fifteen minutes, come get me."

Karpis stepped outside Hannegan's and casually lit a Chesterfield, glancing left to right as he did so. He spotted the man pausing by a trashcan for a moment as if about to toss something out, then seemed to change his mind as he headed off purposefully to his right back toward the downtown area. Laclede's Landing was a long stretch of cobblestone running alongside the Mississippi River leading to a city park due south. It was reasonably lit, though much of the area was covered by shadows at night. Karpis set out in the direction that the man had taken, doing his best to take a circular path so as not to appear to be following him.

As fate would have it, Carole Robbins had gotten off early from work at a nearby restaurant and decided to take a walk along the landing to kill time before she went home for the evening. She had recently relocated from Kansas City in search of a new beginning and a fresh start in life. Carole was a lovely girl with black permed hair, blue eyes, an Irish nose and an hourglass figure. She had been living life in the fast lane for the past few years, hanging around with lots of the gangsters who were still in circulation after Prohibition had ended. She realized that she was on a road to ruin and would need to mend her ways if she ever wanted to find the right guy and have the kind of life she had dreamed of.

She saw what looked like a familiar figure in the distance and could not believe her eyes. It was dark where she was walking and the lamplight provided scant illumination. Yet the sight made her heart leap in her chest, and she could not restrain herself from calling out.

"Ray!" she called at the silhouette. "Ray Karpis! Is that you?"

Karpis spun around and stared at her. He was barely able to recover as the man he was following crept up on him and lunged from the shadows. Carole held her throat in dread as Karpis managed to throw up a cross-block to thwart a downward slash of a foot-long dagger. He threw a right cross and staggered the man, grabbing the knife hand and shoving it to the side. Karpis then kicked the man in the shin, shocking him with the pain so that he was caught off-balance and unprepared to stop Karpis from grabbing his arm. Karpis then twisted the knife inward and threw his weight behind it, driving it into the man's ribcage. It pierced his heart and he managed a strangled gasp before he fell backward and gave up the ghost.

Carole came rushing to his side. "Oh, my gosh, Ray, are you all right?"

"Of all the luck," Karpis growled. "Where'd you come from?"

"Is that any way to speak to me after all this time?" she demanded.

"Do you see this mess I'm in?" he snapped at her. "This sombitch just tried to kill me!"

"Well, what did you do to him?" she insisted. "Did you try to rob him? People don't just come up and try to kill you for no reason."

"Look, you," he snarled, grabbing the knife and tossing it into the river, "don't just stand there, gimme a hand. Help me throw him over the side. The cops'll think he got mugged."

"Ray, the guy's dead. I can't touch him, I just can't."

"I just got outta jail. You want me to go back?" He was adamant. "At least help pick up his legs. Look, how do you know he's even dead? Maybe he hits the water and swims away."

"That's crazy, Ray, you just stabbed the guy," she said, approaching cautiously as Karpis lifted the corpse into a sitting position and pulled him up by his arms. Carole made her way over and lifted one leg before jumping back in horror.

"Ray!" she cried. "What is this shit all over his pants!"

"It must be blood, I suppose." Karpis shrugged. "Look, you gonna help me or not?"

"It's on my dress! You ruined my new dress!"

"Shut up, you wanna get the cops over here? I'll get you a new dress, just help me out."

"Hey, are you two fighting again?"

They heard a familiar voice, turned, and saw Fred approaching. Carole came over to give him a hug before he took stock of the situation.

"I told you this sombitch was up to no good." Karpis nodded at the corpse. "I'll snatch his wallet, and we'll throw him into the drink."

"I don't believe this, he's gonna rob a dead man," Carole said in dismay.

"Shuddup." Karpis scowled at her, ripping the man's wallet from his pocket.

Fred then lent a hand as they hoisted him off the pavement and carried him to the edge of the walkway, slinging him down into the river. They then scurried off with Carole right behind them. By the time they reached Hannegan's, Doc and Campbell were already waiting outside. They exchanged hugs with Carole before heading to the parking lot to pick up their cars.

"Okay, look," Karpis decided. "We'll head back to the hotel and I'll get whatever info I can outta this mug's wallet and get it to my connections. We'll lay low and wait to see what comes from it."

"So did you all break out at the same time?" Carole asked as Karpis ushered her into the passenger seat of the Xenia while the others squeezed into the back seat. "How come there wasn't anything about it in the papers?"

"There's gonna be something when I put you in the river alongside that guy in there," Karpis growled as he slammed the door shut behind her.

"Yeah, sure." She opened her purse and began touching up her lipstick as the Xenia disappeared into the night.

⋳⋚⋳⋚

Early the next morning, Chess Power was picked up by FBI agents at his home and driven directly to his field office in downtown Kansas City for a special meeting. When he got there, he was nearly distracted to find that the persons who scheduled the appointment were Melvin Purvis and the director himself, J. Edgar Hoover.

Chess was able to size up the situation as soon as he walked into the meeting room. Hoover was very much in control, and Purvis seemed almost docile around the martinet. Chess shook hands with him as Purvis, who was seated in a chair across the conference table from Hoover, rose to greet him. Hoover merely nodded as he continued to flip through a number of freshly-typed reports in a thick dossier before him.

"So it seems that Senator Truman barely escaped an attempt on his life by Nazi assassins at his home in Independence in broad daylight the other day." Hoover did not look up as Chess sat across from Purvis.

"Sir, our operatives—" Chess began.

"Special Agent Power, let me point out that this is a top secret meeting that officially is not taking place," Purvis explained quietly. "Mr. Hoover remains unaware of the details of our mission and does not know the identities of our operatives. Rather, he has come here to explain the nature of the Bureau's interest in this matter and the importance of its success as regards our grand strategy and future objectives."

"I'm not sure if you're aware of the level of hostility that this man Truman has built up against our organization." Hoover finally looked up, staring across at Chess. "He's under the impression that we are building our own state police force, an American Gestapo. He's been lobbying against us, and there is a clear and apparent danger that if this man ever finds his way into the halls of the White House in any capacity, he will use whatever power he accumulates against us. To be completely honest with you gentlemen, I myself cannot say that justice was served entirely when he escaped from those Nazi assassins unharmed."

Chess was baffled. "Do you mean to say that we should have showed up a little later than we did?"

"What the director is trying to point out is that we got no credit whatsoever for saving his life," Purvis tried to explain. "Truman is using the incident to cast doubts over our efficiency. He is maligning our efforts to combat subversion and radicalism, both here and abroad, stating that we can't even keep track of the spies among us. He's respected our requests to keep the matter a State secret, even though the press did report gunshots fired near the Truman home and that some bullets struck the residence. It's not keeping him from discussing the incident in the strictest privacy, and of course this discussion has reached the ears of the president himself."

"You would think the man would be eternally grateful for us saving his life, yet all he can do is dwell on the fact that we got there in the nick of time," Hoover thundered. "This is exactly why we must keep the existence of this Triad top secret. If the American public ever found out that a team of Nazi assassins were at large within our borders, we would become a national disgrace. Everything we accomplished by winning our War on Crime would be undone. We must prevent this group from ever surfacing before the public eye, and they must be obliterated so that there is no trace of them to ever be found."

"I can pretty well assure you that the men we have

on this case are not exactly the kind who will—" Chess began.

Hoover resumed leafing through the dossier. "I'm not hearing what he's saying."

"The director is not interested in the minute details of our operation, only that we complete it as quickly and efficiently as possible." Purvis held up a hand. "In this economy, the American public is only interested in results, and as public servants we are being held accountable for every cent being invested in our programs and our Bureau. They expect us to protect and defend our country and our people from Nazism, Fascism, and Communism, and this is a sacred duty. This Triad must be tracked down and eradicated, once and forever, and it will be a thankless task for which we will never be credited. The only ones who will be remembered are those among us who will have earned our undying gratitude."

"I understand completely," Chess replied. "My team is focused and razor-sharp. We're on top of this mission and expect to have things wrapped up in short order."

"Our undying gratitude." Hoover stared at him for a long while before rising from the desk, bringing the meeting to an end.

☙✲❧

Hoover had recently returned from Vienna where he attended an INTERPOL conference, and was invited afterward to a clandestine meeting with a high-placed law-enforcement official from the Reich. Hoover and two of his agents accompanied a team of four German diplomats in a limousine to the Konig von Ungarn Hotel near the Stephansplatz. It was there where they were surprised and delighted to make the acquaintance of SS Reichsfuhrer Heinrich Himmler.

The men shook hands and exchanged embraces, communicating through an SS interpreter who was fluent in both English and German. The SS had rented a luxury suite and had ordered a smorgasbord for their special guests, and the law enforcement czars were escorted by their bodyguards for their impromptu summit meeting. A number of high-ranking SS officers were in attendance, and the FBI agents mingled with them as Hoover and Himmler were left alone in a side room with the interpreter.

"We have been fascinated by your success in battling against communists in your country," Himmler remarked once the men had settled back in two of the majestic armchairs adorning the suite. "As you know, we were involved with a desperate struggle against them before we came to power. We were quite surprised that the restrictions and limitations placed on your agency by your government did not impede your remarkable progress."

"To tell the truth, sometimes it makes it easier to circumvent civil liberties in a capitalist society," Hoover reflected. "When the financial security of the merchant class is threatened, they will defend and protect it by all means necessary. This is why we were so successful in out War on Crime, and this is why we will destroy Communism in America. Even though we are in the midst of a Great Recession, there will always be those who have, and those who have not. Those who have will always make sure that their liberties and property is protected, even if it means sacrificing that of others."

"My only fear is that the communists' agenda may be reflecting our own, which makes it difficult to justify an all-out war against the Reds," Himmler mused.

"This is something Mr. Hitler will have to address," Hoover said curtly. "Should a deep relationship between America and Germany ever develop, we could not harbor the impression or likeness between communists and a close ally."

"Let me ask you, sir." Himmler was curious. "Do you not see your eminent domain principle as being consonant with the communists' abolition of private property? If your Fourteenth Amendment provides for the confiscation of citizens' land, does it not contradict the spirit of your Constitution?"

"Not entirely," Hoover hemmed. "The amendment provides for the due process of law before any such actions are taken. Therefore, any land that is confiscated from those found guilty in a court of law is entirely justified. The law does not confiscate property, the courts do."

"Now those reflect our sentiments exactly." Himmler

beamed. "It is very important that they do not see the State as the authority, but merely the manifestation of the people. I've always admired that slogan, 'We The People.' The Bolsheviks claim they represent the will of the people, but they full well know otherwise. Their police forces are designed only to enforce the will of the State over the people. The FBI and the Gestapo are alike in that we serve to eliminate the enemies of the State, who are ultimately the enemies of the people. You have done a remarkable job in eliminating public enemies such as Dillinger and Alvin Karpis. On our end, we have virtually eliminated Communism by striking it at the root with our Nuremberg Laws and their enforcement."

"Yes, sometimes we are forced to suspend or restrict the rights of lawbreakers in order to put them behind bars where they belong. It stands to reason that, if their rights are being denied while incarcerated, then we are merely accelerating the process by doing so in expediting their arrest and conviction."

"Hear, hear." Himmler clapped his hands. "Although the politicians and the media make it seem otherwise, our people certainly do have a great deal in common. Especially among those of us who are sworn to protect and defend their liberty."

And so they continued to discuss at length their plans for creating the greatest police forces in world history.

CHAPTER 6

Karpis made a few calls and was able to pick up a luxury Lincoln Zephyr on Broadway near the Liberty District before cruising back on the Hwy 40 en route to Philadelphia. He and Carole drove the Zephyr while Campbell and the Barkers took over the Xenia.

"So how was this gonna go down, Ray?" Carole snapped. "You were just gonna slip in and out of town and not even look me up?"

"Hey, look, I already told you, I'm on a job for the feds," Karpis growled.

He would have put her in the car with the Barkers but there was an outside chance they would have killed her, accidentally on purpose. He wasn't sure how he was going to keep his head on straight like this. "I'm on one of these work-release type deals. I don't have time to screw around on this schedule looking up people."

"I'm not *people*, Ray, I'm your girlfriend, or have you forgotten already?"

"I've been on the Rock for over a year. Where the hell'd you think I went, to Hot Springs for my health?"

"It might've improved your attitude, mister."

"Look, shut up for a while and let me think."

She continued to prattle on about her daily existence in St. Louis while he tried to focus on his game plan for Philadelphia. They were probably not as well-known there, so connections would be less solid, though their visibility would be much lower. He would have to draw a bead on local German communities that might be sympathetic to the Nazis, and get some leads on pro-Nazi organizations in the area that might make the Triad feel welcome. He might also find help along the underworld with Italians having problems with the fascists in Italy, or Jewish gangsters whose relatives might have been persecuted by Nazis. All in all, the Triad might just be having as hard a time of it as the Karpis-Barker Gang.

"So, Ray, where are you planning on staying when you get to Philly?" Carole wondered. "They've got some really nice places downtown, so I hear."

"Yeah, well, it's gonna be the usual routine. If things get hot, we may have to cut and run in a minute's notice."

"Are we gonna have to stay in the same hotel with

the others? Can't we at least get a room on a different floor? You should just tell them you don't want to attract attention."

"Yeah, well, I'll be attracting a lot more attention with you than them, for sure."

"That's because my legs are so hot." She smirked at him. "Besides, Doc Barker gives me the creeps."

"I thought you two might have a lot in common intellectually." Karpis managed to keep a straight face.

"What do you mean by that, Ray? Are you getting fresh with me?"

"Look, why don't you mess around with the radio and let me think?" he demanded.

It was a half-day's drive to Philly from St. Louis, and they were all tuckered out by the time they reached the city limits. They drove up to the Hotel Monaco in the Lafayette Building and rented two suites as the valet took care of their parking needs. Campbell insisted on carrying the suitcase with the machine guns so as not to attract attention with its great weight. Ray and Carole took the honeymoon suite while Campbell and the Barkers retired to the double suite.

"Isn't this just wonderful, Ray?" Carole gushed, throwing herself backward onto the king-sized bed and kicking off her heels. Her dark blue dress had hiked itself up past her knees, showing her garters just above her white nylons.

Her perfectly-chiseled legs were too much for any

red-blooded male to withstand and, despite himself, Karpis was on top of her in a heartbeat.

"So you really miss this, Ray, don'tcha?" she teased him as he pulled up her skirt and yanked off his shirt and trousers.

"I'd be some kind of faggot if I didn't."

He snaked his tongue into her mouth to keep her from train-wrecking his fantasy. He entered her roughly to take control, then slowed the pace to a loving caress until she was mewling in his arms. She exhausted herself five times before he finally erupted, ascending into heaven before rolling over and pulling her alongside him.

"Oh, Ray, that was wonderful." She snuggled up against his chest. "You don't know what you do to me."

"Yeah, well, you're not so bad yourself, sweetcakes." He kissed her nose before lighting a Chesterfield. "We gotta do this again sometime."

"How about I take a shower and come right back?"

"How about we order some grub and get some shuteye first?" he grunted, taking a drag and handing her the cigarette. "Look, you go ahead and get your shower while I make some calls."

Carole then proceeded to strip naked, nearly driving Karpis to distraction before she headed off to the shower. He called room service and ordered two tenderloin steaks and fries with a bottle of champagne and a pot of coffee before getting back to business. He dialed up his Dragnet connections to see what they had come up with.

He found that the American Nazi Party had been trying to schedule a rally at the Municipal Auditorium near the University of Pennsylvania but was catching a lot of heat from local Jewish organizations protesting the event. If he could determine who was sponsoring the event, he could find out if the Triad tried to solicit their help. Or even more likely, if he could find out who was trying to blackball the Party, he could get all the skinny he needed. He was told to call back in a half hour, and room service showed up just in time for him to take a breather and clear his head.

They brought the food in on a serving tray and set a table for them as was the custom. Karpis was amused by the room server's difficulty in keeping his eyes off of Carole, who stood by in a black negligee and silk robe waiting for the dinner to be served. Karpis finally tipped the server, who was reverent as a church usher as he thanked Karpis before taking his leave.

"Mmm, this is excellent, Ray." She sipped and savored the vintage champagne as Karpis took a couple of bites of steak. "You may be hard to handle, but you've got the best taste of anyone I've ever known."

He grinned, ending his meal with a couple of bites of French fries. "Yeah, well, I ended up with you, didn't I?"

"That's sweet of you, Ray." She smiled sweetly. "Hey, where are you going? You're not gonna leave me here to eat by myself?"

"What? Do you think I'm going to Pittsburgh?"

Karpis growled. "I'm going into the next room to make a goddam phone call."

"Yeah, and what? To call one of your other girl-friends?"

"And have her talk my other goddam ear off?"

"What's her name, Ray?" she demanded before he slammed the door behind him.

He called Dragnet back and found that the American Jewish Society had been the ones lobbying against the Nazis and had even called in their markers with some politicians in the state congress and Washington. He got the contact information with the leader of the Society in Philly and decided to pay him a visit. In the meantime, he would have Campbell check out the Nazi Party reps here in town, and get the Barkers to take a ride out to the German-American Society. That should cover all bases and have them moving in the right direction at the end of the day.

When he came back out, his dinner was still relatively untouched but her plate and the champagne bottle were empty. He knew she would be in a great mood, and smiled to himself as he headed for the bedroom.

"Ra-ay," she called seductively from the darkened room. "I'm waiting."

"You won't have to wait long, doll face," he said, pulling off his shirt and tie as he closed the door behind him.

And, he decided, neither would the Triad.

ᘓᘉᘓᘉ

Karpis and Carole had breakfast the next morning at the Red Owl Tavern on the grade level with the others, who were in a chipper mood and ravenously hungry as they had not ordered dinner the night before. Karpis gave them their assignments as well as the Dragnet phone number, making arrangements so that they could take and leave messages with the service until further notice. The boys ate their fill as Karpis patiently waited around so they could all leave at the same time.

He drove out to the West Side near Strawberry Mansion which had long been considered the Jewish Quarter. It had been a thriving community until 1924 when congress placed a restriction on immigration from Eastern Europe. The new generation of Jewish-Americans began expanding their horizons in moving out of the community, and the numbers began to dwindle as fewer newcomers trickled in. Yet the Old Guard continued to protect and serve the neighborhood, and they were not about to let the American Nazi Party bring their anti-Semitic policies to Philadelphia without a fight.

Aaron Mandel was a local businessman who had taken the profits from two sweatshops and began investing in real estate in the area. Over the years, he had gone from labor profiteer to pillar of the community, and was elected president of the American Jewish Society. He was a short, bespectacled man with a domineering way about him, and he and Karpis seemed to clash as soon as Karpis walked into his office.

"So what do you wanna know about the Nazis, that they're trying to turn Eastern Europe into one of their goddam concentration camps?" Mandel barked as Karpis and Carole took a seat in his snug yet well-furnished office near the B'nai Abraham Synagogue on Lombard Street. "Or maybe they're going to start one right here in West Philly next. I'll tell you one thing, pal, I got more German friends and business associates here in Philly than you can shake a stick at. They think they're gonna start their goose-stepping parades down Broad Street any time soon, they're gonna have hell to pay first. So what's your story, are you two Germans?"

"No, actually my folks are from Lithuania, and both our moms are Irish," Karpis told him.

"Lithuania," Mandel grunted. "Either the Nazis or the commies'll get them next. Well, how can I help you?"

"We're trying to find out who's in network with these guys," Karpis revealed. "We're doing a private investigation, and we're thinking there's some out-of-town money involved from here in the USA. Do your people know who was funding that shindig, or have an idea of who might want to give the Nazis a jumpstart here?"

"Well, that's a good one," Mandel mused. "In my opinion, if they wanted to rewrite history—which is usually their first step in alienating the Jews—if I was them I'd start off in York County."

"Yeah?" Karpis wondered. "Why's that?"

"If you knew your history, you'd know that William Penn had lured Germans over from the Rhenish Palatinate near the Rhineland at the beginning of the 1700s." Mandel was impatient. "They came in right behind the English in helping Penn colonize this area. They're considered hardworking people and very patriotic. If the Nazis try spreading any of their poison about the Jews in their area and it takes effect, it'll give them that foothold they need to gain ground in the nearby communities."

"Well, I've got my people following up some leads." Karpis rose to leave as they shook hands with Mandel. "If anything comes of it, we'll give you a heads-up."

"Gosh, he seemed so nice," Carole said airily as they headed back to the Zephyr. "It's hard to imagine that those were the people who killed Christ."

"What're you, stupid?" Karpis snapped. "That's how that Nazi crap gets started. And what kinda nice are you talking about? That was one bad-tempered sombitch."

"What's wrong with *you*, Ray?" she insisted. "Why are you defending him if you don't like him?"

"Look, forget it," he growled. "Just get in the car."

Karpis had not considered where his allegiances lay in this situation, and didn't know if he even wanted to sort them out. He considered himself somewhat of an anarchist on a philosophical level, but was apolitical as far as that went. He wasn't prejudiced by any means, as the color green made all men equal. He just knew that if the fascists or the Nazis came into power, they would set up a police state that would put him out of business permanently. America provided for his way of life, and he would take a stand to make sure it was preserved.

Campbell left a message to meet him back at the hotel, and they headed back to the Monaco before making plans to ride over to Ralph's Italian Restaurant on Ninth Street.

They were cordially welcomed by the old country staff, and the waiter took their orders before bringing a couple of bottles of rose wine to their table.

"Okay, here's the deal," Campbell reported. "I talked to the Nazi Party reps downtown, and they told me that they were having some political problems here but were making some moves in York County."

"That's the same story we got." Karpis nodded. "Looks like we're on track."

"That's about what I got from the German-American Society." Fred lit a cigarette. "They've had some out-of-towners asking about the best places for German nationals to live without having to deal with all the political bullshit going around. They've been telling people that York County's the place with the oldest German history in the state. If there's ever a political shitstorm over the crap going down in Germany, York'd be the place to tide it over."

"That makes it unanimous," Karpis replied. "We head out first thing in the morning."

❧❧❧

They checked out at the crack of dawn, and soon both vehicles were on their way to York County near the historic Gettysburg area. They made their way to Route 30 and made their way toward Lincoln Square to the Adams County Winery, where they planned on asking directions to the Battlefield Bed and Breakfast. Campbell picked up a case of their Rebel Red wine, promising to split it with Carole once they got situated. The storekeeper gave them a complimentary map to the Gettysburg Battlefield, and they were soon on their way.

As they approached the Battlefield Bed and Breakfast, they slowed down as they all spotted a familiar face on the side of the road. Standing out in front of Swan Cottage along the drive to the main house was none other than General Dwight D. Eisenhower. They pulled up at the picket fence running around the house and got out to meet him.

"Well, I hope you fellows are having as swell a time as we are." Eisenhower exchanged handshakes with all of them. He was wearing a white shirt and khakis along with a light-colored hat which kept the sun off his head. "Mamie just went up to the main house to get directions. We'd actually come out here to see if there was some property for sale. My folks originally came from these parts, and we thought it'd be a great place to raise our own younguns."

"My buddy here just bought a whole case of wine, and once we drink it, we'll probably think this is a swell place too." Doc grinned as Fred turned away in exasperation.

"Say, uh, General, did you tell anyone else you were coming out here, like anyone you were visiting with?" Karpis wondered.

He saw a late-model car picking up speed as it sailed up the road, and it piqued his curiosity.

"We tend to report our comings and goings with our staff, if that's what you mean," Eisenhower replied, just now catching sight of the vehicle's dust cloud growing larger along the ribbon of road in the distance. "I wonder if someone's got an urgent matter to attend to."

"You don't suppose it's someone coming out here to ask for an autograph," Karpis shielded his eyes from the sun, staring intently at the dust cloud.

"I can't imagine rightly what they'd do with it once they got it," Eisenhower replied.

"I got a funny feeling about this." Campbell sauntered over to the Xenia and nonchalantly popped the trunk.

Once the vehicle came to within twenty yards of the small group, it swerved violently into a U-turn, spraying dirt and gravel everywhere. Campbell threw open the trunk and pulled out the heavy suitcase, setting it on the ground before the occupants of the vehicle hopped out, brandishing submachine guns. They aimed and fired at the small group, all of them diving for cover as Karpis grabbed Carole and the general around the necks before taking them to the ground.

"Carole, go ahead and get that suitcase open, start passing those guns out!" Karpis told her.

She scrambled over to where Campbell was and began giving them out as he passed them along to her.

"Goddam sombitch," Doc growled as a stray bullet tore the sleeve of his suit jacket.

He grabbed one of the Tommy guns and leaped up, spraying bullets so that the gunmen were forced back up into cover behind the sedan—only his gun jammed and he began frantically jacking the chamber as the gunmen began reloading.

Karpis handed Eisenhower one of the submachine guns. "I imagine you know how to handle one of these, General."

The general chuckled. "Never met one I didn't like."

At once, they leaped to their feet and were shoulder to shoulder, assuming the position before commencing fire. Karpis and Eisenhower stood side by side, pouring automatic rounds into the enemy.

The first gunman was hurled backward in a dance of death as slugs tore through his body from head to toe.

He fell dead to the ground in a torrent of blood and lead as his partner jumped into the vehicle and sped away.

"You know the drill." Karpis winked at Campbell

before relieving Eisenhower of his weapon. "Are you okay, General? You sure did give that fellow the old what for."

"Golly, I'm sure glad Mamie wasn't here." Eisenhower dusted himself off. "I'm not sure she would've handled it as well as your lady friend there."

Carole smiled proudly. "We Missourian women are a sturdy breed, General."

"That poor little cottage certainly came out the worse for wear." Eisenhower shook his head as they all stared at the bullet-riddled Swan Cottage.

Karpis gave hand signals behind the general's back, and the Barkers quickly grabbed the assassin's corpse and tossed him into the Xenia.

"Sure is a damn shame." Karpis shook his head. "Sons of bitches out joyriding, shooting up everything in sight. Well, my friends'll drive you up to the main house so you can call the missus and tell her you're fine."

Eisenhower turned toward the road, removing his hat and scratching his head as he stared at the blood trail in the dirt. "Say, I thought we hit that one guy."

"Hell, he jumped up and ran like hell." Doc laughed. "I betcha he's caught up to his buddy by now. Ran so fast my hound couldn't catch him."

"You brought your dog with you?" Carole was wide-eyed. "Where'd he go?"

"Like peas in a pod." Karpis rolled his eyes. "Doc, why don't you and the boys drop the general off at the house, and we'll catch up with you over at the meeting place."

"Well, I certainly do want to thank you." Eisenhower shook Karpis's hand as he and Carole took their leave. "It sure was fortunate that you and your friends came along when you did. Those guns of yours sure came in handy, too."

"Yep, we came up here to do some deer hunting." Karpis smiled. "Never thought we'd be expected to serve our country in such a manner."

Eisenhower grinned. "Say, did anyone ever tell you that you look like Lawrence Tierney?"

"Not recently." Karpis patted him on the back. "It's been a pleasure, sir."

"What a swell guy." the general watched as the Zephyr streaked back down the road. "Actually, I think he looked more like Alvin Karpis, but I wouldn't have wanted to insult him."

"Yeah, that might've ruined his day," Fred allowed.

With that, Campbell and the Barkers dropped General Eisenhower off at the bed and breakfast facility, heading off into the sunny afternoon with the corpse of a second Triad member in the trunk of their Xenia.

இஇஇ

It was almost midnight by the time SS Colonel Richard Haden showed up at INTERPOL headquarters in Vienna, where SS General Kurt Daluege awaited after receiving an urgent call from SS Headquarters in Berlin. Haden, an expert pilot, flew his private plane from the German capitol and was driven from the airport to Daluege's office upon arrival.

"Damn it, Haden, this is as ridiculous as it is impossible," Daluege thundered as the impassive officer sat before his desk. "This is the second botched attempt by our team after thirty straight successes over the past nine years! How in hell could have they known we were trying to assassinate Eisenhower? I would also like to know who these people are! And, moreover, how did Von Hoffman get killed? He was one of our best commandos, ranked at the top of his class in the very first Waffen SS academy course. What kind of squad could the Americans have assembled to cost us such losses?"

"We have been getting strange field reports back from our operatives," Haden revealed, his feline features menacing in the dim light. "Our underworld connections have indicated there is a team of impostors traveling along the network where the Triad has been assigned. There were multiple communications mentioning that the leader of this group bears a striking resemblance to Alvin Karpis, the kidnaper and armed robber who is currently serving a life sentence in the federal prison on Alcatraz Island. Our assumption, at this point, is that this team is impersonating the Karpis Gang in order to avail themselves of his past connections. We are also beginning to suspect that the FBI might have formed this group if they heard rumors of the Triad being in country to carry out an assassination or an act of sabotage."

"It's those Italians, those damned Italians!" Daluege smacked his palm on the desk. "It was one of the worst political blunders this country ever made by getting involved with those people! Mussolini and those fascists are lazy, careless bunglers who are going to end up stabbing us in the back. They are talking about eradicating the Mafia from their society. How can they do that when half of their support comes from the Mafia? Even worse, they are getting their best information from the American Mafia. What makes them think that whatever they find out is not being sold back to this Karpis Gang right after it is reported to the FBI?"

"Unfortunately this is the nature of espionage, my general," Haden said ruefully. "Rats create holes which cause leaks. Every rat eventually outlives its usefulness, and must be exterminated when it causes one too many leaks."

"When we gave the target list to the Triad, we told them the exact reasons why each of the persons of interest was to be eliminated!" Daluege said angrily. "Our psychologists and psychiatrists have carefully researched and analyzed this man Eisenhower. They have no doubt that this man has political aspirations beyond his military career! If we were to enter a war with the United States, this man would attain a comprehensive knowledge of our military capabilities. He would be able to use this as part of his political platform in his bid for power. Like Truman, he will undoubtedly beef up his personal security so that no one will be able to get near him. Colonel, we can afford no more mistakes. This next phase of the operation must prove successful. The success of the Third Reich in the coming months depends on it!"

"The Reichsfuhrer asked me to give you his full assurance that everything possible is being done to ensure that such an unforeseen situation will not keep us from our purpose," Haden advised him. "He sent me here to give you his personal guarantee. This next target will be eliminated as scheduled, and you will have the Americans eating from your hand."

"Very good. Just one more thing."

"Yes, General."

"This Karpis fellow. I want you to send someone out to Alcatraz and make sure that the person who is killing our operatives is not the one who is supposed to be in prison for the rest of his life."

"I will see to it, Herr General."

Haden was picked up by his chauffeur and driven to a nearby hotel for an overnight stay. He would fly back to Berlin and notify Himmler of Daluege's concerns tomorrow afternoon.

He was quite sure that Alvin Karpis would still be in Alcatraz before and after they sent someone over to check.

ೕೋ

Karpis was quite certain he was no longer in Alcatraz, but the story of one Robert Badamo had roused him from his sleep more than once. He wasn't sure where or when he heard the story, or whether it was true or not. He couldn't remember it for sure, and it was another one of those situations where he suspected his dreams were getting mixed up with his real life. He knew that the government might have a way of controlling that. Obviously, they had not before, because they would have caught him long ago. Now that they had Einstein's commitment to what they considered liberty and justice, it could well be possible. He'd have to check his science journals and see.

ೕೋ

Robert Badamo was a recent high school graduate who had gotten a job with the First Bank of Kansas along with a classmate, Deborah Patane. They were both assistant tellers, and Deborah got assigned to her own window within weeks.

Robert got assigned to their new change machine, which somehow could magically count coins. They were poured into the funnel of the grumpy-looking brass-colored beast, and after its great belly jingled and churned, the coins were counted out to the last cent.

People from all around brought their piggy banks in

greater number than storekeepers, just to see how much they had saved up over months or years.

Robert had been embarrassed and humiliated during an incident in which he came up a few dollars short at the end of the day. It was at the beginning, when he first got assigned to the machine. He was fairly certain that the head teller, an absolute bastard named Angelo Vacirca, had skimmed some off the top for a quick score. Most likely it was to improve his position in the contest for Deborah. All the male bachelors, and even some married fellows, had eyes for her. Robert had worshipped her since they were in grade school, and he knew he would have to speak soon or forever hold his peace.

He was preoccupied by thoughts of how he could restore his esteem in Deborah's eyes. He was pretty sure that, even though old Football Head had made him look dumb, it wasn't going to help Angelo that much. He only wished they were still in school where he could hit a home run or make the game-saving catch at an inter-school baseball series. Now that they were adults, or at least in the grownup world, it would be so much harder to set himself apart from the rest. Especially since they were the lowest-paid workers in the bank. The defining moment in his life came when four men walked into the bank, dressed in straw boater hats and tailor-made suits. Though the boaters were all the rage yet quite common, the suits were of a marvelous fabric and fit the men perfectly. They were definitely not from the Sears and Roebuck catalog. Neither were the Thompson submachine guns they produced when they announced they were robbing the bank.

Mrs. Stephens merely rolled her eyes and fainted behind the tellers' window, while the guard had his front teeth knocked out with a smash from the butt of one of the guns. Deborah was greatly upset but no more so than when she got a 95 out of 100 on a spelling test back in school. Mr. Tillson came rushing out of his office but had his tie grabbed and used as a short leash like in a Charlie Chaplin movie.

"All right," the leader, an impossibly skinny young man, announced to the dozen customers on his side of the counter. "This is a stickup. We're here for the bank's money, not yours. You can collect whatever's yours, but I want everybody on their ass on the floor now."

The second man, who had the gaping look of an imbecile, nearly slugged a man for attempting to reach over the counter and take a little extra. The third man, who had the terrifying look of a cold-blooded killer, stepped back and looked about for someone to shoot. The fourth man, who jumped over the counter, was as a chameleon. He looked like everybody else in the bank. He looked like Vacirca—who got butted so hard he almost had a convulsion—like Mrs. Stephens, like Deborah, even a little bit like Robert. He had the most remarkable face Robert had ever seen, yet he would never be able to describe it in a million years.

"Slim pickings, Ray," the chameleon man called to the leader as he emptied the cash drawers into a pillowcase. Everyone knew that the first nook in the cash drawer was attached to the central alarm, but these fellows did not care. The man in the blue suit looked like he wanted to kill someone. The alarm went off, and the women in the bank began praying that they would not be slaughtered. Instead, they were herded together and forced out the door as hostages along with Mr. Tillson. Angelo started to say something but they kicked him in the face.

"Hold on." Robert jumped to his feet as four machine guns were trained on him. "Don't take Debbie. Take me instead."

"Well, then, she's still going, and so are you."

The idiot-looking guy came over and grabbed him by the tie, the way the nuns did when he screwed up at the Catholic grade school he and Deborah had attended. He may have earned the respect of everyone, but must have looked pretty stupid when he was dragged out by the tie into the street, as was Mr. Tillson. They watched as the entire Wichita Police and Sheriff's Department showed up, yet dared not shoot as the hostages were positioned on the running boards on either side of the car. The killer drove the car and the thin man sat alongside him up front. Robert was sandwiched alongside Mr. Tillson between the chameleon and the imbecile as they drove off.

The robbers let loose a stream of automatic fire on the police as they gave chase, causing them to swerve and slow down in their wake. The gangsters told the women to hold each other tightly, and they reached out the window to grab hold of the women's dresses so they did not fall from the running boards. Robert only hoped that Deborah's dress did not tear, or that she did not grow faint and fall onto the dirt road they came upon at length. The killer was an expert driver, and he had them over ten miles away from town within minutes. Robert knew the distance as he had gone fishing out this way since he was a boy.

Eventually, they slowed to a halt beside the old fishing hole, and the killer and the thin man argued over it. The idiot tried to butt in but the thin man told him off. The chameleon produced sandwiches and apologized that there was not enough to go around. He explained that they had driven all night to take this score and hadn't eaten since yesterday. Nobody cared because they were all too distracted, and when the thin man announced they would be let go shortly, they were ecstatic. The thin man had Robert sit right alongside Deborah on the back fender of the car. He decided that one would not run without the other, and it would be easier to take off with two hostages than eight. He also said he would wait fifteen minutes to see if the cops showed up. If they did not give chase by then, they were probably going to let the FBI handle it. The thin man had most likely robbed a million banks and knew this to be like the Word of God.

"Are you okay?" Robert asked Deborah.

Everyone wanted them to be together: their friends, their family, even the nuns at the Catholic school. He had blond hair, blue eyes, a bit pudgy but cute nonetheless. She shared the same attributes, and they would make a lovely couple.

"I'm fine, Robert," she replied, her longish bangs blown across her face by the wind. "That was a brave thing you did, coming with us. You shouldn't have done it."

"I had to do it," he insisted. "I love you, Debbie."

"Why, I love you too, Robert," Deborah managed. After all this time, he had said the words she longed to hear since they were pre-school age.

Robert was speechless. All he could do was bask in Deborah's loving gaze. At once it was if her love permeated the very air. The atmosphere was almost idyllic as the killer walked under a shade tree to eat his sandwich. The idiot was talking to the thin man about his lucky coat, showing it to him as the thin man grunted absently, flipping through his science journal.

The women gathered around Mr. Tillson, asking quietly if they would be walking back to town soon. It was the most wonderful moment of Robert's life. It would have been hard to say if he would have forsaken it, even if he had known about Roy Rodgers lurking in the bushes about fifty yards away from the Studebaker and its passengers.

Rodgers was a Texas Ranger who had come to Kansas after taking part in the murder of Bonnie and Clyde as orchestrated by Captain Frank Hamer. He had heard the Karpis-Barker Gang was up there, and he knew that taking them down would further enhance his career.

Rodgers followed the trail of the robbers from Wichita, and parked his car in a clearing off the road to sneak up on their parked vehicle. He carried with him an M-1 Garand, the high-powered combat rifle that WWI vets said would be Hitler's worst enemy should he choose to run afoul of the good old USA. He saw the hostages gathered off to the far side of the vehicle as the robbers appeared to be resting for their retreat across the state line. He figured that if he got some good shots off, he might take out the gang leaders and leave them in disarray.

The ranger was a crack shot, but he wasn't used to the long-range variables in shooting with the Garand. Plus, the weapon had not been cleaned properly since he left Texas, which would create problems in the best of situations. Rodgers, normally a cautious man, would throw caution to the winds in taking his first shot.

He took careful aim, waited until his target was perfectly still, then fired a shot that shattered the perfect calm of the afternoon.

His bullet ripped through Fred Barker's sandwich, tore through Doc Barker's lucky coat, burned its way through Alvin Karpis' science journal, and hit Robert Badamo right between the eyes.

Deborah Patane thought he was horsing around as he rocked sideways and sprawled dead across the grass. She only realized what had happened as drops of blood, appearing as rubies, fell from his forehead and gleamed in the emerald grass.

Karpis woke in another cold sweat, bolted upright, looking around for the ranger, and found himself in his own bed. "What the—"

Another damn dream.

CHAPTER 7

Bob Feta heard about the incident at the Battle-field Bed and Breakfast shortly after his Irish Mob connections told him that there was a ru-mor of the Karpis lookalike having been seen in St. Lou-is.

He made a beeline to Philadelphia, then on to York County, and was getting little more than yesterday's news until he got in touch with Joe Adonis.

"Okay, it's a good thing we were able to make the connection," Adonis assured him as Feta prepared a string of excuses as to how he had lost Karpis's trail over such a great distance. "He's coming into our territory now. We've got lots of people who know people in Philly, and they'll keep their ears to the ground. These guys'll turn up somewhere, and when they do, we'll put you on top of them."

Genovese's connections in Alcatraz did some checking and found that Alvin Karpis had been in solitary for over a month. The only thing they thought suspicious was that he was no longer playing memory chess with the guards. Other than that, they were delivering his physics books and newspapers to his cell on a regular basis, and his meals were still being returned half-eaten to the mess hall. The gangsters failed to uncover the FBI's careful subterfuge.

"That's the second time they've been on the scene to thwart an assassination attempt," Feta mused. "It doesn't make any sense. First of all, if they were in on the plots, why didn't they just let them happen? Second, why isn't the government spreading the word? None of this stuff is making the papers. They reported the shootout at the Truman house and the bed and breakfast, but neither Truman nor Eisenhower was placed at the scene by the press."

"That's what we're payin' you to find out," Adonis insisted. "Maybe they're sending a warning to the government, who knows? Plus, if somebody had the muscle to target a senator and a general, and threaten the US Government, don't you think they'd want the world to know it? Especially in this day and age, with guys like Hitler throwing his weight all over the place. They want these guys to tip their hand before they make their move.

We just got to make sure that, no matter how it goes down, they don't try and blame it on the Mob, especially Charlie Lucky."

Feta, like the Karpis Gang, had white line fever by the time he reached Philly, but did not have the luxury of being able to rest up and bide his time. Mr. Mulligan had called him shortly after the attempted hit on Eisenhower and ordered him directly to Pennsylvania. Once he got there he called Joe Adonis and caught a catnap before planning his next move. He picked up a couple of sandwiches and coffee before heading to York County and found that the state police had cordoned off the roads leading to Gettysburg.

"Okay, look," Mulligan told him when he called to report the roadblocks near the shooting area. "We got word that the Karpis ringers were spotted in New Jersey. We need you to be very careful and proceed with caution. I don't know where they're getting their information, but they've got to be hot on the trail of that hit squad. I can guarantee you that whoever's paying the freight for that Triad isn't gonna put up with another botched deal. Whoever or whatever their target is, they'll either take it out or die trying. We should have enough info to make sure you're there when it happens. Don't forget, we want proof that the Sicilians are behind this Triad after the smoke clears, so you make sure you get all the information we need."

Feta's biggest concern at this juncture was if the Ital-

ian Mob found out that he was playing one end against
the other with the Irish Mob. If Genovese learned of his
connection with Mulligan, there would be no place on
earth for him to hide. Even worse, if he came up with
proof that Genovese was backing the Triad, it would trigger one of the biggest gang wars in American history.
The Mob would have to rub him out just to keep their
business secret. Yet, if he backed out, he had no doubt
that Genovese would have him whacked.

His stomach was churning with apprehension, but he
had no choice but to wait until Mulligan or Adonis gave
him enough info to move forward. He had to get a solid
lead on this Karpis lookalike and hold on tight. There was
just too much hanging in the balance for him to come up
short one more time.

෨෩෨෩

Once again Karpis had made arrangements to drop
the dead body off with an underworld doctor for an autopsy report, and they picked Atlantic City to get the
work done. The fabulous resort area was controlled by
Nucky Johnson, who was considered the boss of the
City's political machine. Karpis had decided that the
gang would lay low, in order to avoid attention by Johnson's people, but made the fatal error of picking the Ritz-
Carlton Hotel as the place for them to regroup and prepare their next move. He was unaware that Johnson lived

on the ninth floor and had all of the suites set aside for his exclusive use. When his men spotted the group checking into the hotel, they contacted Nucky immediately. It was not long before Karpis was sent an invitation to meet with Johnson on the ninth floor.

"Well, well." Johnson rose from his overstuffed armchair in the luxurious parlor of his main suite to greet his guest. "Alvin Karpis. How in hell were you able to escape from Alcatraz?"

"I'll tell you, Nucky, it's a long story, and I'm in a jam. If I come as clean as I can, you think you might be able to help me out?"

"As best I can," Johnson allowed. "Of course, we'd hope that it might be a profitable arrangement for both of us. What do you think I can do for you?"

"Can we talk somewhere in private?"

"I keep no secrets from my boys." He gestured at the four tuxedoed goons lounging around the suite. "Let's sit up here and have a drink at the bar and discuss business."

The bartender poured Nucky a shot and Karpis had tonic water as they sat at the chrome-trimmed mahogany bar. Johnson was a heavy-set, balding man with gold-rimmed glasses that looked like many of the managers at the countless banks the Karpis-Barker Gang had robbed.

"I'll level with you, Nucky. The feds gave me and the boys a deal. The Nazis have a kidnap gang here in the country, who've made a deal with the Mafia to snatch a bigwig politician here in the States. The feds figure since we're experts in that line of work, we'd be the best ones to put on their tails. Now, I know that the feds have been coming at you the same way they got to Al Capone, with that tax evasion routine. If you can help me out here, I'll bet I can get the feds to go easy on you."

"Say, this can work out great for everyone." Johnson's eyes lit up. "You know those greaseballs have been eyeballing this town since before Prohibition. If you can help the feds prove they're working with the Nazis, that'd help take them down once and for all. Plus, if you can get me off the hook for that tax rap, it'll be a whole new day for me. Tell me, Karpis, what can I do to help?"

"I want to set a trap for the Nazis and the Mob," Karpis confided. "Look, suppose I have the feds put out the word that there's gonna be a big political event here and lots of bigwigs are gonna be showing up? If you help us set this up, maybe we can lure the rats into the cage."

"Just as you say, kidnapping is your area of expertise, setting up major events is one of mine, and something on this scale simply can't be done on such short notice." Johnson frowned. "Of course, to set up a sting operation, you'd need to rely on word-of-mouth and let the marks in on the deal so that they think they came across something big on their own."

Karpis was enthused. "Now you're talking."

"As a matter of fact, word around the campfire is that the White House is staging a big event somewhere along the East Coast to rally support for this new policy they're planning to put into effect. Roosevelt's supposedly gonna make this Quarantine Speech that'll encourage the League of Nations to blackball the Axis Powers if they continue being aggressive toward the rest of the world. If you make the Nazis think they're planning it here, it might do the trick."

"Sounds like a plan," Karpis agreed. "Let me get in touch with the feds and see what they think."

"Be sure and put in a good word for me," Nucky reminded him.

ᴇ⁄ᴈᴇ⁄ᴈ

Fred shook his head as the gang met at Hackney's Restaurant for dinner that evening. "Damn, Ray, I don't know where you get those bright ideas of yours."

Johnson had called in advance and made reservations, asking that the meal be placed on his own tab. The gang was able to pick their own lobsters from the tank at the facility, which were served along with filet mignon and vintage champagne.

Fred and Karpis had an eye for seafood, being expert fishermen, and made sure everyone got a prime choice. Only Carole eschewed the lobster selection, unwilling to eat something that she had seen walking about a short time earlier.

"Well, having Johnson's people put the make on us had a lot to do with it," Karpis said modestly. "He's a pretty smooth operator himself. Having a finger in the political pie around here didn't hurt matters any. If we can catch that Triad in here snooping around, maybe we can ambush them and wrap this job up."

"I'll tell you, Ray, I've seen a few banks in our travels that I'm wanting to come back and take another look at." Fred took a bite of buttered lobster before washing it down with a sip of champagne.

"Are you nuts?" Karpis shook his head. "You think the feds won't be watching us anywhere in the country we go after this? You gotta start thinking about a foreign country. Maybe South America, or even Canada. Europe'll be out once we're done. If we bump off the rest of the Triad gang, chances are we'll be on Hitler's Most Wanted list next."

"What're we gonna rob in South America, *pesos*?" Campbell grunted, cutting himself a juicy bite of steak. "And Canada's too damn cold. You should know, you were born there."

"Why do you think my old man brought us down here?" Karpis replied. "Don't forget, though, it works both ways. If we hit places where the local cops don't have the kind of cars to chase us down in the snow and ice, we might be able to get something going."

"Yeah, like suppose we made a whole bunch of little campfires, from the bank back to our hideout?" Doc speculated. "This way we could warm up and thaw out the cars while we're making our escape."

"I think maybe we oughtta stick with having Ray do the planning," Fred said mildly.

"Why don't you guys pick somewhere romantic, like in Mexico?" Carole wondered, enjoying her shrimp salad. "This way we can mix business with pleasure. You can find a hideout where it's nice and there's lots of places to go shopping."

"I agree with Freddie," Campbell said amiably. "We oughtta leave it up to Ray."

"I don't know," Karpis said glumly. "With all the guys in our line of work either six feet under or in the slammer, the yegg days in this country may be over. We might just want to see how the chips fall after this one and think about going in with the Mob family that comes out on top. I hear they pay their racket guys pretty good these days."

"Screw that." Fred shook his head. "I'll take my chances in South America."

∽∾∽

The abortion doctor's autopsy report was teletyped over to Karpis's Dragnet connections, who came up with an SS Lieutenant Eric von Hoffman. He, like Markoff, had also been in the USA as part of a diplomatic entourage in the early 'thirties. Karpis had the Barkers drive out and pick up the body, wrapping it in a tarpaulin and weighing it down with rocks before dumping it off the

Jersey shore. His next move was to get in touch with Chess Power and tell him about the meeting with Nucky Johnson.

"I think you're right on the money with this, Alvin," Chess said, enthused. "Army Intelligence may have a double agent working on this case. If he can spring a leak, making the Nazis think the Atlantic City Convention Hall is gonna be the place for Roosevelt's speech, maybe your idea'll work. Tell Johnson we'll be good to go with this."

"How about you guys putting a good word with the tax man for Nucky?" Karpis asked.

"Well, you know what they say about death and taxes, but I certainly will give it a shot."

Karpis next got in touch with Johnson, who was already arranging the ersatz rally. He made a reservation for the hall and had scheduled a set-up so that anyone stopping by would see that work was in progress for a large event. As agreed, he told no one of what was transpiring, leaving it to Karpis's connections to leak the information into the underground by way of their double agents.

It was not long before the Genovese Family's people caught sight of the Karpis lookalike around the Ritz-Carlton, and they immediately notified Joe Adonis who contacted Cat the Bounty Hunter.

Feta made a beeline to Atlantic City and found a small motel just a couple of blocks from the Boardwalk before he called Mr. Mulligan to let him know what was going on.

"Okay, that's just fine," Mulligan reassured him when Feta filled him in on the details. "I want you to keep a close eye on those ringers, but be very careful. Nucky Johnson literally owns that section of the City, and his people are always on the lookout for suspicious characters. They've been worried about the Mob muscling in on their operations for decades. If they get the idea that you're connected, they'll put a tail on you that you won't be able to shake off. Your best bet is to get yourself dressed up like a tourist and spend as much time in your hotel room during the day as possible. You know the routine, if you think you're being followed you probably are. If you get something sticking to your tail that you can't shake, you give me a call and we'll see if I can't get it off for you."

Soon the word along the underground was that President Roosevelt himself was coming to Atlantic City for a rehearsal speech at the Convention Center. It was to be a black tie affair, invitation only, and some of the most important politicians and dignitaries along the East Coast were scheduled to attend. The Genovese Family put out inquiries but was astonished that they could get no further information about the event beyond what was being leaked.

They chalked it up to the fact that the president was attending and dug no further, lest they run afoul of the

Secret Service and any other federal agencies involved.

Nucky Johnson's next move was to contact a local actors' guild and put out a casting call for a major motion picture sequence requiring stock actors to participate in a crowd scene along the Boardwalk area. They were to meet at the Convention Center at a specified date and time, and were to remain on alert as the parts were going to be assigned on a first-come first-serve basis. The guild directors warned Nucky to expect a mob scene in this economy, but Johnson assured them that everything would be just fine on his end.

The stage was now set for one of the biggest sting operations in Atlantic City history. The only concern of the Karpis-Barker Gang was whether the Triad would take the bait.

℘℘℘

The curiosity of both Vito Genovese and Kurt Daluege, as well as that of the entire population of Alcatraz Island, was to be satisfied at the crack of dawn as all the prisoners were summoned to the yard where a large platform had been erected overnight by the guards. The giant spotlights along the walls shone their great lights on both the platform and the two hundred and fifty inmates, most of them cursing and swearing at the brightness. "There have been rumors circulating that one of the prisoners on this island has escaped and, by some grand cover-up, no one in this facility is aware of it," the warden announced on the microphone hooked into the institution's public address system. "Prisoner Number 325-AZ, Alvin Karpawicz, has been in solitary confinement for numerous violations of our code of conduct here at this prison. During this phase of corrective punishment, he has been kept clear of interaction with the general population. We believe that these bizarre rumors have been started because of this restriction."

With that, Warden James Johnston made a grand gesture, and a feeble man of average size was prodded out from stage right into the spotlight. The man appeared malnourished, his uniform hanging on him, and he shielded his wire-rimmed glasses as he faced the audience.

"Behold the man!" the warden exclaimed into the microphone, holding his hand out in the prisoner's direction. "This is the prisoner known to most of you as Alvin Karpis, who was once considered by law enforcement to be Public Enemy Number One. This puny shadow of a man was once regarded as a symbol of rebellion here at Alcatraz and, as we can now see, he has responded favorably to correction and will be returned to the general population."

Character actor Mayo Caceres had been arrested for the manslaughter of his wife two years earlier, and authorities had taken note of the fact that he bore a strong resemblance to Alvin Karpis. He was transferred to the

Rock and was offered a deal to impersonate Karpis in exchange for having his life sentence commuted to twenty years.

His story was that he had developed amnesia in the Hole, which would offset attempts by fellow inmates to verify his identity.

He would also claim that his fingertips grew back so as to dispel doubts that he was the printless bank robber.

At length the prison yard began filling with mooing and lowing, as the sound of disconcerted cattle. The warden's face grew mottled with anger until the mooing became intolerable.

"Silence!" Johnston roared as the microphone squealed with the violence of his voice. The sudden quiet was next broken by the cacophony of shotgun shells being jacked into their chambers by the guards that surrounded the prisoners along the prison walls.

"Prisoner!" the warden yelled in his face as he lowered his head with fear and trembling. "What do you have to say for yourself?"

"I firmly resolve, by your grace and mercy, to turn from my rebelliousness, to learn from my mistakes, and to become a model prisoner here at this great and terrible prison," the man replied timidly.

"Go then," the warden pointed to stage right, "and sin no more!"

As the prisoners were dismissed, many watched the dismal little figure leave the stage with disgust. More than one of them would go throughout the day wondering what it was that broke the spirit of the man once considered an invincible underworld legend.

CHAPTER 8

The Convention Center was bustling on the big night, with a large black-tie crowd milling around outside the facility. The police and press were alerted to what appeared to be an impromptu event, but Nucky Johnson's people politely informed them that it was a private affair off-limits to the general public. In Johnson's town, that was sufficient to ensure the utmost confidentiality.

As the doors were finally opened to accept the guests, they were greatly impressed by the cavernous hall, illuminated by enormous chandeliers glittering with thousands of zircon-like crystals. White linened tables set with china dinnerware, polished silverware, floral arrangements and candlesticks bracketed the carpeted dance floor, over which presided a great dais with matching podium and long table, behind which sat an orchestra pit. It was almost as if out of a movie, and only the money and power of Nucky Johnson could have set such a thing up in so short a time.

Only, Nucky himself was filled with trepidation as a group of makeup artists crowded around where he sat at a dressing room mirror. His hair was being tousled and powdered and his face painted before a pair of metal-framed glasses was propped onto the bridge of his nose.

"Hey, this is never gonna work!" Nucky argued, trying not to panic. "You guys are nuts!"

"C'mon, Nucky, do it for your country," Karpis handed him a pair of metal crutches. "From the stage with all them lights, nobody's gonna be able to tell the difference. You'll look just like President Roosevelt."

"What's all this stuff about Nazi spies anyway?" Nucky insisted as the gang led him toward the entranceway leading to the great stage where all the tuxedoed actors had gathered around in what appeared to be a standing-room only crowd. "Suppose somebody takes a shot at me? Why don't you let somebody send out for a bulletproof vest?"

"Look, you're already carrying a few extra pounds as it is." Fred grabbed his shoulder and guided him toward the stage curtain. "If you put on a vest, you'll look like a walrus, and no one will believe that you're Roosevelt."

Nucky grabbed the crutches and hobbled out onto the

stage, his eyes wide as quarters as he stared into the lights, expecting a bullet at any moment.

There was a round of applause and smattered cheers as the President of the United States was introduced by the master of ceremonies.

"Those aren't very good actors you got, Ray," Carole noted, looking over Doc's shoulder. "They don't even yell and cheer for the President of the United States."

"What do you think this is, a football game?" Karpis growled. "All right, Harry, get out the machine guns. Let's make sure if anyone puts one in Nucky, we fill 'em full of lead."

"Say, those are great-looking machine guns you got there," said one of the makeup girls who came over to where the gang was waiting in the wings. "They almost look like the real thing."

Fred walked over and tilted it around. "Well, I'll tell you, doll face, why don't we go over there by the couch and I'll show you how things work?"

"C'mon, Freddie, we're in the middle of something here," Karpis insisted.

"See that?" Fred griped as the makeup girl reluctantly walked off. "It's always business with you."

"My fellow Americans," Nucky Johnson began, reading the prepared statement, "I am glad to come once again to Atlantic City and especially to have the opportunity of taking part in the dedication of this important project of civic betterment."

"Why does he keep jacking around with the notes?" Campbell wondered.

"I think they might have slipped him the wrong kind of glasses," Karpis decided.

"Why don't they just call 'Cut' and do the scene over, like Fred Astaire and Ginger Rogers?" Carole wondered.

"We're not making a movie, we're trying to catch Nazis," Karpis growled. "Now pipe down for a while."

"On my trip across the continent and back I have been shown many evidences of the result of common sense cooperation between municipalities and the federal government, and I have been greeted by tens of thousands of Americans who have told me in every look and word that their material and spiritual well-being has made great strides forward in the past few years," Nucky finally pulled the glasses down so they sat on the tip of his nose. The gang could scarcely keep from laughing as they saw the notes shaking in his hands.

Suddenly, the doors to the Center were kicked open at the grand entrance, and a squad of gunmen came barreling into the facility. "Kill the president!" a voice called out.

"I'm not the president!" Nucky cried, throwing the notes and the crutches aside. "I'm not the president!"

"C'mon, Nucky, you're ruining the show." Karpis ran out and hauled Johnson away before a storm of bullets ripped across the podium. At once, the gang charged out from backstage, returning fire at the gunmen as the actors ran screaming for cover.

"Damn you, Karpis, they're shooting up my arena!" Nucky yelled as automatic fire continued to splinter the polished wooden stage floor.

"You tryin' to tell me you don't have insurance?" Karpis insisted, lying on his belly as he began crawling toward the edge of the stage. "Aren't you in good hands with All State?"

The gang had taken cover behind the row of seats vacated by the actors onstage as Carole joined them in running for shelter. Campbell and the Barkers began spreading out from right to left, their Tommy guns chattering as they forced the enemy agents to cower behind the seats at the rear of the theater. The gang jumped off the stage and raced toward the front row before resuming their volley.

Karpis rolled over into a sitting position and began spraying bullets at the attackers, giving Johnson a chance to break for the backstage area. He next rolled across center stage and tumbled off onto the floor, darting toward the front row where he began moving right in an attempt to outflank the riflemen.

He could already see the others moving left, and the assassins were calling to each other in German in an attempt to counter the attack.

"I'm not sure this is a good idea, Ray," Fred called over as both sides began reloading their weapons.

"There's about ten of them and there's four of us. Maybe they can't shoot worth a damn, but they've got lots more ammo than we do."

"Maybe you're right," Karpis replied, his eyes darting around as he pondered his next move. "I'm gonna make tracks toward the far wall, cover me."

"There's five guys on your side, Ray," Fred warned him.

"They can't shoot worth a damn, remember?" Karpis winked before he popped up and made a beeline for the wall to his left. Suddenly the area was shredded by gunfire as Karpis ducked and dodged, bullets causing plaster and wood chips to fly everywhere. He took a flying leap and smashed the glass cover over a small box on the wall, punching the red button inside before diving to the carpet. At once a bell began clanging as the Nazis stared in wonderment.

Doc looked around quizzically. "Lunch time already?"

"That's the fire alarm, Ray," Campbell yelled at Karpis. "This place's gonna be crawling with cops!"

"Well, at least they're not gonna be looking for you," Karpis called back.

The Nazis realized what was happening and began abandoning their positions, covering each other's retreat as they backed out of the auditorium. The gang waited until the last two gunmen took their leave, and Fred jumped up and cut them down from behind.

"C'mon, guys." Karpis beckoned to them. "Let's get the bastards!"

"Be careful, Ray!" he heard Carole cry out.

He looked up onstage and saw her amidst a large group of actors and stagehands who had come out from backstage as soon as the coast was clear. Karpis winked and blew her a kiss before leading the charge out the doors in pursuit of the Nazis. Doc started to take the wallets from the pants pockets of the dead men but Fred pulled him along to join the chase.

They followed the assassins out the door, and once again the Nazis turned and sprayed bullets at their pursuers. The gang ducked behind the pillars and posts near the entrance, returning fire as Campbell cut down one of the fleeing gunmen with a volley across his back. He tumbled and rolled down the stairs as the other assassins continued running for cover.

They could hear the sounds of sirens, and suddenly there appeared a great number of lights in the distance, indicating the police and the fire department were on their way up the boulevard toward the Convention Center. The spies were taken aback as to what to do, and the Barkers took advantage in cutting down another man with a spray of bullets. The remaining six men broke into a panicked run, fleeing down the steps in the direction of the approaching vehicles.

The police cars slammed on the brakes at the sight of the armed men, throwing open their doors and pulling their guns as they ordered the assassins to drop their weapons. The Nazis, realizing they were surrounded, saw no choice other than to fight their way out.

Karpis rallied the gang along the steps, calling them back inside the facility as the Atlantic City Police began firing on the foreign agents. Within minutes, the gunmen were lying dead on the sidewalk before the Convention Center, riddled with bullets.

"All right, guys, let's get these choppers back in the suitcase and move on outta here!" Karpis told them as they ran back inside.

Only, they stopped short as they faced a dozen rifles aimed at them by police officers who had come in through the rear entrances of the building.

"Okay, you men, hold it right there and drop those weapons!" the ranking officer ordered.

"Hey, take it easy, you guys." Karpis laid his weapon on the ground as did the others. "We're some of the actors Nucky Johnson called out here. We started doing this scene and all of a sudden these guys started firing live ammo. We need to get these guns back to the studio to make sure nobody switched out our blanks for real bullets."

"Hey, fellows, he's on the level." Nucky came running down the aisle toward the officers. "They sure are with the acting troupe we called down here. They were surprised as everyone else when those damned Nazis came in here and started shooting up the place. If they plan on coming out here to Atlantic City and start taking over, well, they got another think coming."

"Say, this guy looks just like Alvin Karpis," one of the policemen marveled.

"The hell you say," Karpis growled. "I'm Lawrence Tierney."

"Hey, guys, it's Lawrence Tierney," the cop said excitedly. "Do you think I can have an autograph for my wife? She loves your movies. She's seen every one."

Another cop produced a pen and paper. "He was only kidding about you looking like that ugly dog Karpis."

Nucky was joined by Carole as the gang came over, Campbell gathering up their machine guns and putting them away in the suitcase. They then waited patiently, laughing amongst themselves as Karpis signed every last autograph for the grateful policemen.

~~~

Chess Power had scheduled an appointment earlier that day with Thomas E. Dewey, the Manhattan District Attorney. Dewey had not only sent Lucky Luciano to prison a couple of years earlier, but was building a case against Albert Anastasia and his Murder Inc. assassination gang. The DA's Office had imprisoned contract killer Abe Reles and got him to turn state's witness against his former colleagues in order to escape the electric chair. Lepke Buchalter had been arrested along with some of the gang's most notorious killers, and Dewey was certain that Reles's testimony would allow him to take down Anastasia next.

"So it looks like you've got those Mob guys on the run," Chess said airily as he sat back in the armchair before Dewey's desk in his spacious office suite. "You know, we've been looking into those shooting incidents in Missouri and Pennsylvania, and we're trying to make sure they're not gang-related. We're just hoping it wasn't a coincidence that two high-profile leaders were identified as being in the proximity of the areas where the gun battles occurred. If those Mob guys are looking to change the shape of the country's future by eliminating potential candidates for office, we aim to nip it in the bud."

"Well, you may be glad to hear that we think we've got enough on Buchalter to send him straight to the electric chair," Dewey replied.

Chess thought it amusing that the DA resembled J. Edgar Hoover with a mustache.

"We've got a few more of his boys we're planning to fry right behind him," Dewey continued.

"You wouldn't be coming across any interesting tidbits about the American Nazi Party?" Chess wondered. "You know how it is, with all that political turmoil in Europe. The director tends to think that some of those Nazi sympathizers here in the States might be thinking along the same lines as those gangsters. If they think they can knock off one or two of our leaders, they'll figure they may be able to weaken our resolve if they decide to start shoving our allies around."

"As a matter of fact, I've got a fellow named Fritz Kuhn who's behind the eight ball as we speak," Dewey said enthusiastically. "Mayor La Guardia's investigating his German-American Bund for tax evasion. It's looking like we're going to be taking him down for embezzlement. Those Nazi bastards came in strong at their rally in Madison Square Garden back in February, but all they did was paint a target on their asses. It won't be long before we shut them down."

Chess smiled broadly. "I think that this is certainly something the director will be pleased to hear."

He realized that this was undoubtedly painting the Nazis into a corner. With the Mob on the run and the Bund facing elimination, the Triad would have no one to turn to if their assignment led them into New York City. The trap was set, and it was only a matter of time before the predators went for the bait.

He only hoped that the Karpis-Barker Gang would be able to prevent the Triad from changing the course of history.

ᏯᏋᎧ

Karpis had a dream that he had been put in the same cell with the Devil.

Only, he was a strange looking little man, about five-

foot-five and weighing as much as Karpis. He woke up
and saw the Devil seated on a bunk across from him,
which made no sense because none of the cells provided
for two occupants.

"Say, uh, I heard you were pretty good on the guitar,
and you sing okay too," the man said in a friendly,
though nasal, voice. "I was kinda hoping you might be
able to check out some of my stuff, see what you think."

Karpis sat up on his cot, rubbing his eyes. "Who the
hell are you?"

"Name's Charlie Manson. I just got transferred here.
I've been playing guitar in the yard and a couple of peo-
ple mentioned your name. They say you sing like Elvis
Presley."

"Yeah? Well, I mostly play just to pass the time.
What kind of stuff do you do?" Karpis couldn't remember who Elvis Presley was.

"It's kinda like folk rock. I do mostly originals. I
wanted to get your opinion on one of my songs. I think it
has potential."

"Well, I'll give it a listen." Karpis nodded at his guitar propped in the far corner. He didn't know what folk
rock was, either, and wondered if this fellow was all
there.

Charlie got up and retrieved the instrument, then
tuned it slightly as Karpis tried not to frown. Most people
couldn't tune worth a damn and he would have to go and
retune it when they were done.

"Cease to exist, come and say you love me," Charlie sang. "Give up your world, come on an' be with me. Submission is a gift, give it to your lover. Love and death, is all for one another…"

Most of the song was about love and death, and some of it sounded suicidal. Karpis was reminded of some of the stuff going around in the psychiatric journals, about Freud's theories on sexuality being manifested in dreams of death. It was consonant with C.G. Jung's own dissertations on meaning and interpretation of dreams as expressions of subconscious dissonance. Maybe this Manson kid was ahead of his time.

Charlie finished with a flourish. "Well, what do you think?"

"Not bad, kid."

"I've heard tell you've got some connections in Vegas." Charlie got up and returned the guitar back to its place. "You think you might be able to put in a good word for me?"

Karpis wasn't quite sure about what kind of impression this kid would make in Vegas. He needed a shave and a haircut and most likely would have to change his taste in clothes. He didn't look like the kind who would put on a tie before he went out at night. He definitely wasn't the type Karpis would send to Meyer Lansky with a personal reference.

"Well, I'll tell you, kid, my best suggestion would be to hit the club scene around LA and Frisco and get some stage time. I'll go ahead and send a couple of letters out, and you can keep in touch when you get out. Once I get something firmed up, we'll go from there."

Charlie sighed, lying back down on his cot. "I was thinking about going out that way and getting in touch with the Beach Boys."

Karpis was still wondering when they put him in here, and how the hell another bunk got in here without his knowing. It had to be another one of those government mind-bending tactics. No way he was going to let on that he had noticed anything out of the ordinary. Screw them.

"I can really relate to their music," Charlie continued. "I'm gonna try and get hooked up with Dennis Wilson and see if I can get something going."

"That sounds like a plan," Karpis allowed.

This kid kept bringing up these bands and musicians like they were something special. Karpis was pretty well up-to-date on popular music, and he was sure he had never heard of any of these people. It must have been some of that weird Bohemian stuff.

"That's the worst part about being in here, time keeps dragging on, like the song." Charlie stared at the ceiling. "They're out there killing presidents, putting men on the moon, and we're in here just frozen in space. It kinda makes you feel like killing everybody when you get out. Don't you feel that way sometime?"

"You know, kid, it sounds like you came here from

another planet." Karpis stared at him. "Where are you getting all this information from?"

Charlie looked back at him. "How long you been here, fellow?"

"Well, let's see…1936, that's…erm…"

"Holy cow, you been here over thirty years!" Charlie was startled. "That sucks!"

"What the hell?" Karpis exclaimed.

He sat up at once, blinked his eyes, and found the room had gotten completely dark. He was surrounded by shadows and the sights and smells were completely different. He felt a rustling next to him and nearly jumped out of his skin.

"Ray!" said Carole's sleepy voice. "What's wrong now? Go back to sleep."

"Holy crap." Karpis wiped the sweat from his brow. "Carole, what year is this?"

"*What*?"

"I asked you what year is this."

"Ray Karpis, what the hell is wrong with you?"

"I asked you a goddam question!"

"It's 1939, you danged screwball! Now lay down and go to sleep!"

"Geez." he dropped back and pulled her over by his side. "I just had a dream I was back on Alcatraz, in a cell with the Devil."

"Yeah?" She snuggled up to him. "What did he look like?"

"He looked like a goddam bum. He said his name was Charles Manson."

"Never heard of him." She rubbed her little nose on his pajama top. "Go to sleep."

Karpis closed his eyes, hoping he would never hear of him again either.

CHAPTER 9

Madison Square Garden remained the greatest arena in the world, still thriving even in the midst of the Great Depression. The New York Rangers hockey club, the New York Knickerbockers basketball club, and local wrestling and boxing organizations continued to book the facility regularly. Other groups that frequented the fabled hall were Ringling Brothers and Barnum and Bailey Circus, as well as dog shows and evangelical rallies.

The political rallies were no exception, as even the American Nazi Party had planned to book a couple of days to stir up support for their cause. Yet on this occasion, the appearance of President Roosevelt came as a great surprise to the residents of New York City. There had been no advance notice of the event, and it had only been spread by word-of-mouth as Garden workers were the first to learn of it.

Much like the gathering in Atlantic City, the black-tie affair was attended by dignitaries from all walks of life, though none were actors as those at the Convention Center. They were invited for a preview of Roosevelt's Quarantine Speech, which would be a turning point in American foreign policy, even though the USA would maintain an isolationist stance abroad.

Though Hitler, Mussolini, Stalin, and Emperor Hirohito were professing non-aggressive philosophies, world leaders were wary of their imperialist policies and reluctantly braced for military conflict. Roosevelt's viewpoint was that they should all be isolated in carrying the plague of war.

Karpis was one of those dressed in a tuxedo as he entered the arena along with Carole, Campbell and the Barkers. The arena floor was covered with rows of chairs as at a musical concert, with the stage set as at a convention with the speakers' platform dominating the dais. Campbell had brought along the cumbersome suitcase, along with a special pass provided by Chess Power that permitted him to haul such luggage about.

"Where are we supposed to sit?" Carole wondered, resplendent in a white evening gown and heels.

Campbell and the Barkers also wore tuxedos, and Karpis noted amusedly that they glanced at every window and mirror as if to reinforce their belief in what they saw.

"We'll be about five rows from the front," Karpis replied, shooting his cuffs as he perused the upper levels which were slowly filling with guests. "I'll be on the lookout once this thing kicks off, so the rest of you just enjoy the show. Don't forget, now, because we don't want to have the whole damned arena watching us case the joint."

The affair finally began as a number of prestigious political figures from Tammany Hall took the stage. The NYC political machine was out in force, showing support while flaunting their power before the influential federal government representatives. Mayor Fiorello LaGuardia was among the elite, with crowds flocking around to exchange handshakes as he ascended to his reserved seat onstage.

"That'd be the guy to kidnap." Fred nodded at LaGuardia as he continued to wave from the stage at the cheering crowd. "I bet they'd pay serious money to get him back."

"Well, you know these politicians." Karpis shrugged. "They might pay you even more to keep him."

Eventually, the program got under way as a councilman opened the show with a speech about how immigrants had come to America under the torch of the Statue of Liberty at Ellis Island, seeking a new life in the promised land. Next was a State Representative addressing the concerns of second-generation Americans finding their identities in their country by birth. He was followed by the Little Flower, as the mayor was called. LaGuardia delivered a rousing speech in which he gave a scathing rebuke to criminal elements that had come to America trying to establish illegal enterprises similar to those in their countries of origin. He let the enthusiastic audience know that foreign entities seeking to corrupt the truth and justice of the American way would be thwarted and ultimately defeated by the American people.

They had a marching band on the podium that served to enhance the pro-American ambiance of the event, and they went into a half-dozen patriotic tunes that brought the audience to fever pitch. After a very brief pause, LaGuardia himself resumed the platform.

"Ladies and gentlemen," he proudly announced, "the President of the United States!"

The gang reluctantly stood along with the rest of the crowd and joined in a standing ovation as Franklin Delano Roosevelt walked up a short flight of steps to the podium. It was well known that the president had been crippled by polio for over a decade, yet he fought valiantly behind the scenes to make it seem as a hindrance he had overcome. He had specially-constructed "legs of steel," braces that kept his legs from collapsing as he moved to and fro with the aid of metal crutches. It gave him a robotic motion as he made his way to the podium before a standing ovation even greater than that accorded the Little Flower.

"My fellow Americans," Roosevelt began, "I am glad to come once again to New York City and especially to have the opportunity of taking part in the dedication of this important project of civic betterment."

"For crying out loud," Fred snapped at his brother, who was craning his neck backward and gawking up into the upper mezzanine. "Ray's doing the eyeballing, why don't you turn around and enjoy the show?"

"I thought I saw a Nazi guy," Doc insisted.

"Look, you," Karpis growled, "quit making a scene. This guy's the President of the United States. You gotta pretend to show respect."

"You know, Ray, *you're* the one making a scene, quit talking!" Carole insisted.

Karpis had enough of Carole rebuking him all day. "Now see here—"

"I did! I did!" Doc was exultant. "I did see a Nazi guy! He's right up there!"

"Holy smoke!" Karpis whirled around and saw a man in black attaching a stock from a small attaché case to a long-range rifle as he crouched in an alcove at the end of a sparsely filled row on the first mezzanine level. "Harry, quick, the Tommies!"

Karpis realized that, in order to get this job done right, they would have wanted to set up a moving triangle with their target set dead center in the middle of it. There had to be a second shooter, and he gazed in amazement at the opposite end of the balcony where yet another man dressed in black was in process of assembling his own rifle. Karpis next stared at the upper seats behind the bandstand and could see a third man on the upper level, working feverishly at something behind the balcony ledge which Karpis was certain was another sniper rifle. "I'm gonna save the president!" Karpis told his partners. "Harry, pass the Tommies! Carole, hit the deck!"

"Ray, if you mess up this show, I'll never speak to you again!" Carole hissed at him.

Karpis jumped up from his seat and charged up the aisle, vaulting up onto the podium where he was intercepted by a Secret Service agent. Karpis dropped the agent with a hard right, and suddenly had agents charging him from opposite sides. At once he heard shots ringing out from the upper balconies behind him, and the two agents fell to the ground with gaping chest wounds spilling blood across the floor.

"Duck, Mr. President!" Karpis yelled, tackling the president high around the shoulders and knocking him backward to the floor. Two more agents rushed over, hauling Karpis off the president and turning the pulpit over on top of Roosevelt. Karpis was pleasantly surprised as the steel-plated pulpit acted as a turtle shell for the president against which bullets bounced harmlessly.

"Hey, that's swell!" Karpis said admiringly. "Think there's room for one more in there?"

"Beat it, Karpis, you rat!" an agent growled. "Find yourself a hole in the wall!"

By now Campbell had passed out the machine guns, and the gang was drawing a bead on the snipers raining down automatic rifle fire onto the stage. The audience was fleeing in terror, this attack seeming to be the real thing as politicians, not actors, were running for their lives. Some of the overweight and elderly members of the audience had keeled over, and men were doing their best to drag swooning women to safety. In other cases, women were doing their best to drag their obese husbands away.

"Ray!" Campbell yelled, grabbing one of the submachine guns by the barrel and swinging it as a tree limb in as high of an arc as he could. Karpis made a diving catch, hitting the deck as he rolled across the ground with the Tommy gun safe in his arms. He regained his feet and looked upward, catching sight of the third rifleman as he watched and waited for the surviving agents to pull the pulpit up from where the president lay. Karpis opened fire, and the riflemen jerked stiffly before flipping face-first over the railing to the arena floor.

Karpis then looked over to where Carole was trying to regain her bearings, watching in alarm as the Barkers and Campbell exchanged shots with the snipers, who had the gang pinned down in a crossfire. He jumped off the stage and walked up onto the back of one of the front row seats, using the rows as stepping stones to reach where Carole was hiding.

She was flushed with anger. "Ray Karpis! Here we

are, our first time at Madison Square Garden together, listening to a speech by the President of the United States, and you pull a stunt like this!"

"Okay, look." He pointed to an emergency exit. "I want you to go through that door and down the street to where the Zephyr is parked. You pull it around here and wait for me to come out behind you."

She gazed into his eyes and touched his cheek. "I love you, Ray."

"Yeah, right," he said, then gave her a peck on the lips before jumping up and firing at the snipers who were crouched down behind the balcony walls. Carole got up and made a dash down the aisle to the emergency exit as Karpis covered her escape.

"Alvin Karpis!" one of the snipers called out in a German accent. "You have led your gang to their doom! Throw down your weapons and we'll let you leave here alive!"

"Yeah? Bullshit!" Fred jumped up, pouring automatic fire at the metal rail above where the snipers were hiding. The bullets began ricocheting wildly. One of the riflemen tried to escape but lost his equilibrium and toppled over the rail. The second gunman also tried to vacate his position, losing his grip on his weapon as he dropped dead from a head wound.

"Nice work, Fred," Campbell said admiringly.

"Guess I haven't lost my touch," Fred said modestly, buffing his fingernails against his lapel.

Karpis handed Campbell his Tommy gun in exchange for a revolver. He started trotting toward the exit and caught sight of a tall man in a tuxedo running toward the double doors. He was going to drop him but thought better of it, deciding to follow him outside instead. He broke through the double doors and ran down the concrete corridor to a dimly-lit exit sign. Karpis slammed through the doorway and found himself in a side alley, spotting the Zephyr about fifteen yards away. Only the tuxedoed man was with Carole, holding a gun to her head.

"All right, Karpis," Emiliano Murra snarled in a guttural Sardinian accent. "Every game must come to an end. Drop your weapon or your girlfriend will die."

"If you kill that girl, you die next," Karpis insisted, squaring off into a three-point stance, holding the pistol grip in both hands as he aimed at Murra's head.

"Do not test my resolve, Karpis," Murra snarled. "Drop the gun or the bitch dies."

"Who are you calling a bitch!" Carole was irate, stomping down with her high heel as hard as she could on Murra's instep. Emiliano's eyes bulged with pain, providing Karpis with a perfect target. He aimed and fired, hitting Murra right between the eyes. The Sardinian dropped like a felled tree, splashing in a mud puddle behind Carole.

"Ray, are you crazy?" she gasped. "You could've got me killed!"

"Why don't you give it a rest?" he snapped, handing Murra's gun to Carole before rifling through his pockets and yanking his wallet loose. He pulled the bills out of the fold before tossing it down into the corpse's face. "C'mon, let's scram!"

A car pulled up alongside the Zephyr and hit the brakes for a split second. Karpis looked and saw Bob Feta in the back seat behind the man he knew as Jack Mulligan. Only, Karpis recognized him as Chess Power, who winked and waved before driving away.

Karpis and Carole climbed into the Zephyr just as the Barkers barged through the emergency exit ahead. Campbell was right behind them, towing the heavy suitcase along with him. Karpis gunned the engine and pulled up alongside them as the gang piled into the back seat. With that, the Karpis-Barker gang took off, regretting that they would never receive the thanks of a grateful nation.

CHAPTER 10

Karpis yawned and stretched, basking in the sun at his beachfront property on the Costa del Sol in the Torremolinos section along the shoreline of Spain. It was considered a low-income fishing village at best, with most of the locals barely making ends meet in local industry. Just as Karpis figured, he could live like a king in such an area and earn enough loyalty and respect to ensure his privacy throughout the community.

He and the gang got their early release from Alcatraz as promised. They were told that ringers would be substituted in their place among the population, lifers whose resemblances were enhanced by plastic surgery. As Fred had already been reported as dead in the newspapers, there would be no need to further obscure his whereabouts. It was further decided that Doc would be reported to have been killed during a prison break. Rumors abounded that a small group had been planning it for months, so the Barker ringer would be shot with tranquilizers and transported from Alcatraz without further ado. Only the Karpis and Campbell substitutes would have to be established, and most of that could be remedied by intermittent visits to solitary confinement. Everyone knew you never came out from the Hole as the same person, so most likely the switch would never be proven.

Just as they said, the Barkers decided on going down to South America while Campbell opted for Canada. It was an emotional farewell, as much as one might expect among hardened yeggs, the best in the business. Karpis particularly felt sentimental about saying farewell to Fred, who was his oldest friend over twenty years. They all agreed to keep in touch through their Missouri contacts, but Karpis knew that none of them would keep that promise.

"I got us some margaritas, Ray, and made yours without alcohol just like you like them," Carole cooed as she brought a tray out from the *hacienda* and set it down on the beach table between their recliner chairs.

She had turned out to be the perfect homemaker, finding nirvana in the $50,000 villa he purchased for them. She walked around in form-fitting sun dresses and bikinis most of the time, and they spent a goodly amount of time enjoying their midday *siestas* together.

"I also brought out your papers," she said.

"That's swell, doll."

He smiled as she set his copy of the *New York Times* and the *Wall Street Journal* out, along with Einstein's latest articles in the *Journal of the Franklin Institute*. He was really getting into physics and knew that it would be a worthwhile pursuit in his golden years.

Einstein was coming up with great new theories and he was sure that there would not be many dull moments in years to come.

"So you coming across anything good in there?" she asked, lying down on her chair as she slipped on her sunglasses. The cool sea breeze ensured yet another idyllic day ahead.

"Yeah, they're carrying on about this new quantum theory that Einstein has been pushing," Karpis put on his glasses as he opened the *Franklin Journal*. "There's talk about developing a super bomb that can blow up an entire city. They're thinking that if they can find a way to split a uranium atom, it might set off a chain reaction to produce what they call an atomic explosion. Einstein's trying to get Roosevelt to start work on one so we'd have something to make Hitler think twice about taking over the world."

"*We*?" She giggled. "You're still thinking like an American, Ray. If I recall correctly, they just kicked you out of the country."

"Yeah, well," he grumbled. "I'd sure like to get a

hold of one of those bombs. Can you imagine the kind of money I could ask for?"

"You're one of a kind, Ray." She smiled as she picked up her *Chess Power, G-Man!* pulp fiction novel. "Like Freddie said, always thinking about business."

"Nuclear terrorism." Karpis laid his journal down and closed his eyes. "Mark my words, it's the wave of the future."

And so Alvin Karpis became the first criminal in history to begin plans for hijacking a weapon of mass destruction.

About the Author

John Reinhard Dizon was born and raised in the Cobble Hill section of Brooklyn, NY. He participated in local and high school sports at Bishop Loughlin MHS and was a key figure on the Brooklyn rock scene during the Punk Revolution of the '70s. Relocating to San Antonio, TX, in the '80s, he moonlighted as a pro wrestler before pursuing a BA at UTSA and degrees in Korean martial arts during the '90s. He currently lives in Kansas City, MO, where he is studying for his MA in English at UMKC. Dizon has been studying and writing about American and European society and culture for over twenty-five years.

www.ingramcontent.com/pod-product-compliance
Lightning Source LLC
Chambersburg PA
CBHW061152170626
46809CB00003B/1065